—Praise for—

THE BAR HARBOR FORMATION

"This is a terrific novel about an important moment in American history--when the old families, rooted in both grand tradition and powerful prejudices, were beginning to die out. A wonderful read for anyone but especially for anyone who loves the Maine coast as much as Ann Rutherfurd Austin clearly does."

—David Burnham, Author and former investigative reporter *NY Times*

"The irresistible force of a young woman's self-discovery meets the immovable object of bone-deep family tradition in this coming-of-age novel, a vivid portrait of a vanished time when old money ruled Bar Harbor. Ann Rutherfurd Austin traces a half-century of change with an unerring but compassionate eye."

—Joanne Omang, Former *Washington Post* reporter, editor, foreign correspondent, and author: *Incident at Akabal*

THE BAR HARBOR FORMATION

A Novel

Ann Rutherfurd Austin

ISBN: 978-1-947758-14-8

Designed and produced by
Indie Author Books
12 High Street, Thomaston, Maine
www.indieauthorbooks.com

Printed in the United States of America

For my family

THE BAR HARBOR FORMATION
TABLE OF CONTENTS

PROLOGUE

And even if you were in some prison the walls of which let none of the sounds of the world come into your sense—would you not then still have your childhood, that precious kingly possession, that treasure-house of memories?
Rainer Maria Rilke, *Letters to a Young Poet*

Agnes opened the door and led her through shadows to an unfamiliar room where they sat dressed in cobwebs: her grandmother, her son, was that Aunt Pru in the corner? Others too, unidentified. Perhaps her mother. Maybe her father. And Ian. They sat silently on the faded chintz furniture and watched her.

Katherine Morse dreamed about the dead for years and then finally they left her alone. But it had been nice to see them again if only in the underwater murk of her sleeping memory.

Finally she had stopped dreaming about the house too.

Decades ago, before anybody was dead, all summer every summer, summer after summer, they came to the great shingled, turreted, dormered, and balconied house above Frenchman's Bay. With its treasures and delights, its happy rooms, its forbidden staircases, its scary places, and its secrets, it was more than a house. Some houses are just temporary roofs over one's head, some are projects to be fussed over and then abandoned, and some are Real Estate. But there are houses, particularly the houses of childhood, that are whole worlds, and when the house is gone, it is like banishment, and life afterwards is lived in exile. Burnmouth was such a house.

A hierarchy of family members from stately grandmother to tiniest cousin-in-arms came to Burnmouth to escape the summer stupors of Chicago, Boston, and Philadelphia in the days before air-conditioning. Their pets came too: different dogs over the years, and an occasional cat. A parallel hierarchy gathered in those months, it was known as "the Household." There had once been a butler and a chauffeur, and then the imperious Agnes, with her wound-around gray braid, headed the Household. She ruled over the other maids, the cook, the laundress, seamstress, gardener, the children's nurses, and the college-girl baby sitters. Each year she had fewer subjects.

CHAPTER 1

THE GARDEN PARTY

White lilac bowed
Lost lanes of Queen Anne's lace,
And that high-builded cloud
Moving at summer's pace.
Philip Larkin, "Cut Grass"

Everyone in the "Summer Colony" came to the McAllister's garden party that soft July afternoon. Some left their cars in various postures as though trying to square the grass circle at the front of the house, and some parked behind the tall cedar hedge at the servants' entrance. When those spaces were taken, the drivers, after leaving their passengers, drove back up the driveway to where the old garage had burned in the Great Forest Fire of 1947. The very old ladies told their chauffeurs they weren't planning to be long and not to stray far. The uniformed men gathered and smoked, leaning against an ancient Lincoln.

The McAllister grandsons had been ordered to direct guests down the path to the garden. Swatting bugs, smelling the faded bridal wreath bush behind them, they hoped not too much in the way of etiquette would be expected. Sebastian, the smallest and therefore the cutest, kept tossing handfuls of gravel into the air, and Rex, the biggest, kept pulling him out of the way by the back of his tiny gray jacket.

"Well hello, dear, how nice you boys look."

"Such an attractive necktie."

"What a lovely afternoon, aren't we lucky!"

The path led the tottering guests down beside the huge stone foundation of the house and deposited them onto the great lawn; then the lawn continued to slope to the beach and the bay.

But first came the frilly rectangles of the formal garden and, at the end of these, thank God, was the bar.

Katie, the oldest McAllister grandchild, wasn't among the greeters. Nor was she one of the girl cousins passing cucumber sandwiches and peanut butter canapés. In her bedroom high above the lawn she was still trying on one dress after another, until her bed was piled with the bright pastel flowers of summer cottons, the stripes of jersey and seersucker.

That summer when Katie was fifteen, the furniture of her life still seemed in place. At least as far as Katie knew. Like a bug on a leaf she had no sense of what the rest of the tree was up to. She frequently eavesdropped on the grown-ups' conversations but paid attention only occasionally. Yet this summer something was different, for this summer the opposite sex had finally discovered Katie.

Behind her back some of the grown-ups had been wondering lately whether Katie would be a Great Beauty like her grandmother Eleanor Lewis Bradford McAllister. An hour earlier in a bigger bedroom down the hall her parents had been discussing this very subject.

"No, not a Great Beauty," said her father. "Katie's face is too fluttery. She is on the edge of being beautiful, but doesn't quite make it."

Zack Bowman liked looking in the mirror. He stretched his neck turtle-like as he watched himself knotting the Liberty print tie with subtle brown, tan, and pale yellow flowers on it.

His daughter took after him, he thought; a feminine version of himself, she had his dark wavy hair, full lips, and deep dark eyes.

"Just as well," said her mother as she clipped on pearl earrings at the dressing table. "All my most beautiful friends have led unhappy lives."

"Perhaps Katie will flutter on the edge of an unhappy life," he said.

"Good Lord, I hope she will have a very happy life."

"At least she's a good dancer."

"Oh, honestly, Zack." said Nancy.

Nancy didn't want to discuss it anymore. She felt a pinch of dread as she dressed for the party. In very few years her daughter would have to make the biggest decision in a woman's life and it was so easy to make it wrongly. And in the meantime, who knew what would happen.

Katie thought if she came through the basement playroom she could emerge into the garden without people noticing. Her mother was listening to a gentleman in red trousers delight in the brass and mahogany fittings of his new sailboat.

"I agree. I don't think I could ever like a fiberglass boat either." Nancy McAllister Bowman, tall, sandy-haired, and handsome, didn't have the sort of looks that inspired flirtation. Very different from her daughter.

Nancy tried to concentrate on the new boat owner and whisper to her daughter at the same time.

"Katie, dear, that dress. Don't you think...?"

The new boat owner was among those who claimed that Nancy Bowman was the most knowledgeable female sailor on the island and if lost in a storm he would want her at the helm. Because Nancy dutifully kept her eyes on his flushed face, Katie was able to slide past her peripheral vision.

Katie headed for the cloth-covered bar, white against the deep woods. Its symmetrical flower-filled vases made it look like an altar and its bartenders like priests. In fact these priests often heard confessions; because they worked at the Club they knew their parishioners well. They had only to verify that Mr. or Mrs. So and So wished the "usual" to hand over the proper drink.

Katie surveyed the gathering while she waited for her ginger ale.

Margaret Louise van Linden, a famous writer of mystery stories, sat plopped on one of the few stone benches, her ivory-handled cane dug defiantly into the grass, her bosom a proud mountainside ascended by roads of pearls. Her grandchildren—girls in fluffy dresses, white socks, and Mary Janes, boys in sailor suits—stood behind her, scrutinizing the McAllister cousins from afar.

Granny McAllister, her ankles swelling over her big white shoes, made her way on Uncle Peter's arm over to her dear friend and eased herself down next to her. Katie wondered how far the bench's lion-clawed feet would sink into the ground.

"How brave to have a party outdoors, Eleanor," said Mrs. van Linden into Granny McAllister's hearing aid.

"Once the ferry goes in, it won't seem so private out here," said a gentleman in a well-worn panama hat. "Better to take advantage this summer."

"When do they think they'll have it finished?" a lady asked a gentleman who was expected to know such things.

"Not for quite a while. They've only just surveyed the site."

"Imagine. All those tourists trooping through. People from Canada and Lord knows where else."

"I can't imagine it will affect the McAllisters that much. I mean, it's still two properties away."

"It will probably make horrible noises at ungodly hours."

"On the other hand," said someone, "the town is desperate for the revenue, after the fire."

Our territory invaded, thought Katie.

"Why, hello, Katie," said a lady. "How pretty you look. Is that one of your mother's dresses?"

The first and the last of the ones she had tried on, Katie's new black dress suddenly felt as conspicuous as a gorilla costume. Katie blushed as the van Linden grandchildren glowered at her and more than a few grown-ups stalled their conversations to have a quick look.

The publisher of a famous liberal newspaper, thin and elegant with a silk ascot at his throat, stood ignoring his wife while his eyes sought out the pretty young things over her well-coiffed head. The publisher had sucked off Katie's earring the other night when they danced at the Club. When he handed it back it had been all wet. Now Katie turned away.

Katie had heard that they were a Jewish family and therefore somehow different from the rest, but no one had ever explained why. Of course they didn't go to the Episcopal Church, or the maids' church certainly, but it was something more than that. Perhaps they were more intelligent, better dressed? She wasn't sure.

Katie caught sight of her father surrounded by young people at the edge of the woods. She was struck as always by how handsome he was, how dapper (she liked that word), not tall but very neat; he looked like someone who could tap dance. Katie couldn't hear Zack regaling his youthful audience with a theory about local history but she could see a pretty older girl and some boys were listening to him intensely. Katie could see that his eyes were mostly on the pretty older girl.

"You know, where we now stand was once a quiet fishing village," he told his eager listeners.

He thought it the perfect topic for this summer garden party. "Then at the end of the nineteenth century, summer people began to invade."

The young people liked the way he made summer people sound like Visigoths and Huns.

"First artists and writers came looking for beautiful scenery and solitude, then professors and clergymen and other solid type people came. They lived very humbly, appreciated nature. They were called 'rusticators.'"

The young people smiled at the word "rusticators."

"But then came the millionaires," said Zack ominously, "The millionaires built million-dollar cottages and million-dollar clubs, dressed for dinner, and gave extravagant parties," he paused. "No rusticating for them."

Zack laughed and the young people laughed, too. An enigmatic smile lingered on Zack's face and his listeners wondered what Zack's own thoughts were about all this.

And were there any rusticators at this garden party? The young people were tempted to look around. Artists, writers, professors, clergymen, solid people, or only millionaires?

Whether Katie's own scrutiny had some magical power, or whether he was looking for rusticators, one of the boys did turn around, saw Katie, and smiled at her. She had never seen him before. He wore the summer uniform of white pants and navy blazer, but wore it with a sort of precision, not all rumpled like most boys she knew. He was very good looking, perfect features as far as she could tell, neat black hair, large dark eyes. The smile he gave made her blush and when she took her ginger ale her hand was shaking.

A sudden voice made her jump.

"Want to go down to the beach?"

Michael Blake's white shirt had escaped his belt and an effort to batten down his cowlick had been unsuccessful. One of his sneakers was untied.

"Sure. Nobody will miss us."

The last two summers Katie had decreed one of the unsuspecting summer-people boys as her "boyfriend," and this summer it was Michael Blake. The summer-people boys were only just emerging from what her mother called the scuff-and-mumble age, but they would have to do, because Katie couldn't wait forever.

Katie also chose a popular song to enhance her experience, like a sound track in a movie. Now it was "Blue Moon," because there had recently been a blue moon, two full moons in one month.

"A blue moon," Aunt Pru had said. "You know what that means."

Katie didn't know, but she wasn't going to humor crazy Aunt Pru by asking. Enough that it was like getting more than you actually deserved, something extra. Now as she and Michael slipped down through the tall grass at the edge of the lawn, the tune dutifully began playing in her head.

The ocean side of the high-tide line was public property so perhaps that was why there was no easy way to get down to the beach. Nobody ever used the beach besides the McAllister children anyway; you couldn't swim or eat its mussels, clams, or fish because a pipe funneled their poo right into the water. The children regarded this fat rusty cylinder with awe.

Stumbling along through the rocks, the two were out of earshot of the party now. Only sea gulls could hear Katie's question.

"Want to see Tattoo Island?"

"What's Tattoo Island?"

"Where I used to give tattoos to the other children. I'd make a design with charcoal on a flat stone and press it to the—"

"Naw," said Michael. "Let's go up to where the ferry dock is going to be. I want to see if they've started."

Nancy Bowman wondered where her daughter had disappeared to in that obscene black dress. Nancy had abandoned the red-trousered gentleman and was traipsing as gracefully as she could amidst the other guests; her high heels sank into the grass and angled her backwards as she stopped to greet people. Of course it was happening to the other ladies as well; she hoped the party wasn't ruining too many expensive shoes.

Perhaps it was just as well that Katie was off somewhere. Nancy wondered how many of her mother's friends had noticed the wildly inappropriate get-up on the overgrown child. The dress was cut much too low, nearly exposing the tops of those brand new (but quite lovely) breasts, and showing much too much of her long legs (so like her own). And black on a lovely summer afternoon! And lipstick! And all the other girls with scrubbed faces in pretty pastels. Luckily Carrie, her other child, understood these things, at least so far. Her two daughters were so different.

She must try not to worry so much. Katie might be something of a rebel but Nancy believed in her daughter. Nancy had given a lot of thought to this business of "adolescence," a new concept since her day. It was as though a happy little girl was exchanged for a totally new person. But certainly it was just another "phase," and summer crushes on "cute boys" were an apprenticeship for future wives. Of the few professions open to women, marriage, with children, one's own house to decorate as one liked, and parties to give and to go to, was clearly the best. Otherwise one might have to become a teacher, a secretary, or a nurse. She couldn't imagine Katie becoming any of those things! Yes, the business of puppy love was the beginning of it all, even if the "love" involved only back rubbing and occasionally knocking one's tight lips against another's. Or so Nancy hoped.

Nancy caught a glimpse of her own younger sister, Prudence Burton (also inappropriately dressed, but in the other direction, a mountain of gypsy shawls and skirts over clunky sandals) making a group of teenaged girls, which included Carrie, squeal with laughter. Good, thought Nancy; Carrie so seldom laughs.

The McAllisters liked to joke that the weather was Pru's doing and Pru actually seemed to believe it was. The grown-ups were amused by Prudence's nonsense and didn't mind the children thinking their aunt had magical powers, that her sitting in paper pyramids and eating seaweed and drinking cabbage juice gave her meteorological influence. "Vibrations." Pru explained everything by "vibrations" that she alone was sensitive enough to detect. Little did her family know that Pru was an ambassador from a culture yet to come.

In any case, thank God for the lovely weather! Every conversation Nancy had had began with a variation of that sentiment.

Traversing the lawn alone only for seconds, Nancy was accosted by a tipsy Billy Patterson who suggested yet again that they abandon their spouses and run off to Nova Scotia together. His nonsense always cheered Nancy and she began to enjoy herself.

Late afternoon was everyone's favorite time of day. Many had earned this reward by a vigorous tennis game, a trek up Sargent Mountain, a brisk sail with the ocean stinging the face, or the serial concentrations of the golf course. Perhaps in the morning some had worried about the stock market, or the new cook, or Monday's call from the Boston doctor about the "suspicious lump." Perhaps some had only worried how they could face the same people chattering the same inanities as at all the other parties, but in their second gin and tonics all worries dissolved.

As they stood clutching their drinks among the flowers, bees, and butterflies, a soft July sun slanted in between the tall trees, reminding them that the summer was still young and full of promise. The scents were lovely, too: a potpourri of roses, phlox, pine, cedar, bayberry, and the sea. The water lay placid, blue and gentle, stretching out to Bald Rock and beyond to where the islands slumbered like the giant porcupines after whom they were named.

CHAPTER 2

IAN

It was one of those rare smiles with a quality of eternal reassurance in it, that you may come across four or five times in life. It faced—or seemed to face—the whole external world for an instant, and then concentrated on you with an irresistible prejudice in your favor.
F. Scott Fitzgerald, *The Great Gatsby*

[W]ith cheeks into each of which a flush had come.
Henry James, *Portrait of a Lady*

When Katie and Michael returned it was dusk and the party was over. They tried to sneak in through the playroom but they couldn't get the swollen door open. At the top of the path Michael's father was waiting alone in his car listening to a Red Sox game. It was one of two cars left next to the grass circle. Katie couldn't hear what his father said when Michael climbed in, but the car made an angry screech as Mr. Blake gunned the accelerator and they sped off in an explosion of gravel.

The mud on Katie's new dress was tan against the black cotton.

People would think the worst, disappearing like that, when all they'd done was to climb up the slippery rocks to where the ferry dock's foundation would be. When Michael had tried to kiss her she had turned her head. Under the stone arch in front of the big door she worked at scraping off the mud with her fingernails.

Kate smelled the familiar whiff of stale woodsmoke when she pushed the heavy door all the way open. Seeing so many pairs of eyes on her Katie thought she should have gone in the servants' entrance and up the back stairs. It was a big front hall, bigger than most living rooms, and the group was sitting on velvet chairs and a sofa with needlepoint pillows. Her grandmother, parents, her father's friend Mr. Brooke, and two young men were all looking up at her. One of them was the boy she had seen earlier, the one who had turned around from laughing at her father's witticisms.

"Katie, dear, come and meet Mr. Brooke's nephew and his friend," said her grandmother, beckoning with her beautifully groomed hand around whose thick arthritic wrist a circle of tiny diamonds sparkled.

Mr. Brooke and the young men rose.

"They've been waiting for you, precious," said her mother, patting the sofa next to her. She didn't seem angry, but she was good at acting.

"I am lucky to have my nephew Tommy and his pal Ian Douglas as my summer houseguests," said the jovial Mr. Brooke, bowing like someone in a play as he made introductions.

David Brooke had been Zack Bowman's best friend since they were both hairy-legged chorus girls in the "Hasty Pudding Show" at Harvard, and they were still like teenaged boys, always twinkling their eyes and winking as though they were up to no good. They'd attempted various business ventures together over the years, none of which had worked out. Mr. Brooke's eyes were slightly glazed from many gin and tonics, but twinkling as usual. Katie offered her hand to each, thinking that it smelled of dead clams and other sea gunk, and the two young men shook it in turn. Nobody appeared to notice Katie's dishevelment except her father. Naturally, her father would. He sat in an armchair, knees crossed and smirking at his bobbing loafer. As usual he wore no socks.

Katie perched on the edge of the sofa and tried to sit up straight. She tried to put her hand over some of the mud on her skirt before she dared to look up at the boys. Tom Brooke, tall, blond, and gawky, had that summer look. He obviously drank a lot of beer and was happiest in a boat, on a tennis court, a golf course, or behind the wheel of a fast car.

But Ian Douglas, the shorter and darker of the two, was different. For one thing he wore a beautiful aqua tie (was it silk?) that dangled down as he sat with his hands on his knees, completely relaxed, completely still. He seemed at home—"poised" was the word. He smiled at her as though she were a curious but attractive specimen of some sort, and she felt herself blushing. She looked down again.

"The boys wondered if you'd like to go off to the movies with them," said Mr. Brooke making it sound like an invitation to take a spaceship to the moon. Katie felt herself blush even hotter.

Because the movie wasn't until nine there was time for chatter and explanations, so they discussed how Tom was applying to college and Ian was tutoring him. Ian had been a class ahead of Tom at boarding school and would be off to Princeton this fall.

"Ian is a whiz at math," said Mr. Brooke, as though this was the most amazing talent on earth; certainly none of their other acquaintances could possibly be a "whiz at math."

Katie liked the way summer tutors swelled the pool of possible boyfriends. Everyone knew that unless they were excessively stupid, most New England boarding school boys were accepted by Ivy League colleges, particularly if relatives had gone there. But still, in some cases a certain amount of fine-tuning was required so as not to embarrass anybody. Local wisdom had it that each spring headmasters called the Harvard admissions person, who would ask "How many?" and off that number would go to Cambridge in September. Even Katie's father had gone to Harvard, though it took him forever to graduate. ("Too many parties," said Mummy.)

Katie was delighted to be asked to go to the movies.

"I think I should change first," she said in a voice that was more high-pitched than usual.

"Oh, don't bother," said Mr. Brooke. "That's a lovely dress you're wearing."

"It is," said Ian. "It's wonderful," and there was that smile again, and again her blush.

And so began Katie's introduction to sexual longing.

People liked to say that the Club had "peaked in 1911," when a band played every day at noon, but now in 1950 it would be hard to think of the present generations as deprived.

It was sunny and beautiful the day after the garden party, so the McAllisters ate lunch on the Club lawn. The snapping of the flag, the ringing of its rigging against the pole, and the shrieks of splashing children surrounded Granny as she sat at a round iron table under an umbrella, isolated in spite of her hearing aids. On her wrist the circle of diamonds sparkled where she grasped the wooden armrest. The breeze couldn't stir her dark red hair because it was marcelled into flat curls under a barely visible hair net. Even though she was in her late seventies, it was her natural color. Not that a McAllister woman would ever have dyed her hair anyway. Her crossed ankles made the skirt of her light blue tweed suit too short for a posture more appropriate to long dresses, but the grandchildren treasured her inviting lap and didn't mind seeing the tops of her rolled stockings.

Grinning nervously, she made tiny sucking sounds as her family pulled up director's chairs around her. She loved her family more than anything in the world and she was proud to have her friends like Margaret Louise van Linden and Winifred White see her with them, but still, three children, three spouses, and nine grandchildren multiplied the possibilities for disasters.

The breeze had no trouble agitating the long scarf wound around Aunt Pru's neck. Occasionally it spread the scarf over her face, leaving nothing to see above the neck but her spiky hair.

"Stop it!" she would reprimand the scarf, hitting it down. In her voluminous Hawaiian muumuu she didn't look at all like the other women at the Club—nor did her husband, Uncle Oliver Burton, even though he was a lawyer, look like the men. Though most of him was hidden behind the *Wall Street Journal*, his arms and legs announced that he was wearing a rumpled dark business suit. Occasionally something editorially egregious would cause him to emit groans of disgust and his canvas chair to wiggle vigorously.

Nancy, on the other hand, fit into the summer scene perfectly. Like her friends she dressed in bright summer colors: yellow, apple green, and aqua; linen trousers, a cotton blouse, and a cashmere sweater over her shoulders. Her sneakers were as white as paper napkins and at the backs of them little balls like buoys kept her socks from sliding inside. She was doing her usual needlepoint, which she carried in a linen bag with NBMcAB appliquéd on the side.

"Katie, dear, tell us about the movie last night. How did you enjoy Tom and his nice friend?"

"What did you say, Nancy? Tom and his what?" shouted Granny. She kept fussing with her hearing aid and it kept objecting in loud whistles.

"Tom Brooke's friend. I asked Katie if she enjoyed going to the movies with them."

Just then the town's own whistle shrieked that it was now noon so Katie waited to answer.

"They were okay. I had fun, I guess," she said.

"I thought the other one, Ian I think his name was, was terribly attractive," said Nancy. "Beautiful manners."

"God," said Pru. "Beautiful manners. The pinnacle of human endeavor."

"Shush, Prudence," said Uncle Oliver.

Two nurses uniformed in white seersucker delivered Sebastian, Petey, and Mary, the littlest McAllister children, shivering in wet bathing suits. The nurses put their rejected sweaters on the iron table and retreated back to the Kiddie Pool.

(People under ten were allowed to come up for lunch, but only for lunch, with their families at the Big Pool.) Everyone except Uncle Oliver and Granny got up and moved their chairs back to enlarge the circle.

Katie hoped no one would ask her anything more about last night, so as soon as she had repositioned her chair she went back to reading Hemingway's *For Whom the Bell Tolls* (in four years she would be as old as the heroine, and the year after that not even a teenager, a horrible thought). From the corner of her eye she could see two small male figures playing tennis, one tall and blond, one short and dark. The dark one, his shots strong and accurate, stayed fairly still. The blond one was bounding all over the court like a drunken giraffe.

Zack Bowman headed for the McAllister family from another tennis court, racquet in hand, slapping his cheek with the end of a towel. He had probably won as usual. Passing a waiter he called out, "A double bacon cheeseburger, very rare, and a chocolate malt."

"So how did you like your escorts last night?" he asked Katie, a complicated smile on his face.

"They were okay."

Behind her father came Mr. Brooke, huffing a bit; they had been playing singles. His face was pink and his smile big and expectant.

"Katie, the belle of the ball! I hear you had a grand time at the movies!"

What was he talking about? Tom and Ian had hardly spoken to her. Tom had driven them to the Criterion Theatre and back afterwards. The boys had bought popcorn and Ian had offered his once. Katie had refused and that was the extent of it. Or almost. As he held out the popcorn box just before the lights dimmed, he smiled his wonderful smile again. And he winked. Then the Criterion's curtains with the weeping willows became transparent, jerkily opened to slightly distorted martial music, and huge black and white soldiers somewhere on the other side of the world marched across the screen. After that Katie tried to concentrate on Humphrey Bogart and Lauren Bacall for over an hour.

"She's blushing!" laughed her father poking his elbow in Mr. Brooke's ribs. And then Katie understood how these two overgrown boys had been plotting like meddling old ladies to get their teenagers together.

One of the many ways Zack Bowman irritated his daughter was that he and Dave Brooke made no secret of their fascination with young women. Sometimes watching tennis matches or waiting for luncheon cheeseburgers Katie saw them chortle and snort as they scrutinized some long-legged blonde in a white tennis dress or a two-piece bathing suit. Often the objects of their attention were hardly older than Katie. And she particularly disliked it when their object was her best friend, Jo. Jo, with long straight hair the color of wheat, and arms so perfect she could wear her simple gold bracelet above the elbow.

Katie was jealous because she adored her father. He looked like a movie star, somewhere between Gene Kelly and Cary Grant, and had a way of making the world seem fresh and funny. No one told jokes better than he did, though sometimes they were a little bit dirty and sometimes a little anti-Semitic.

He was always embarrassing Katie. When she'd only just started getting "the curse" he bought her a big box of Kotex (she didn't dare go into the store and buy it herself) and carried it, not in a bag, but naked on top of his head down Main Street to the car where she sat waiting.

As for business, it was probably not that he wasn't good at it, but that he didn't think business would be fun. Thus there were always overdue bills to pay and it even got to the point that only the manager of the Club would accept his checks. They squabbled a lot, he and Nancy; from the time she was little Katie could hear them at night when she was trying to sleep. And yet he never stayed angry. After one fight, he grabbed a kid's water pistol and put it to his temple. Even Nancy, who had been furious, laughed.

Once though, she had seen him cry. That was when the town sheriff had come and driven his car away.

"Sorry, Mr. Bowman," said the sheriff. "We had no choice."

It was because of some bill he had forgotten to pay, Nancy said.

Nancy said he was spoiled because he was the youngest after four sisters and "responsibility is not his strong suit."

He had once told Katie he married Nancy for her money. He'd tossed off this unsettling remark as though he were discussing which beer he liked to drink. It was as though he'd never bothered to learn what fathers shouldn't tell their children, as though he was so charming it was okay if he skipped the whole thing about being a proper father and husband.

But Katie knew he loved her, his oldest daughter, deeply. Once when he was morose he told her that she, Katie, was the best thing he ever did.

Driving Katie home that afternoon Zack told her, "You know, kiddo, Tom Brooke's mother is related to the du Ponts. Huge estate outside Wilmington. Lot of dough there."

"So?" said Katie.

"So, little Miss Know-It-All, you might want to be nice to him. It's not long before you come out. A gal needs a lot of support in the stag line."

"I'm only fifteen, Daddy."

"Three years go fast, before you know it you'll be out there on the market, competing with all the other gals."

"Besides I think Tom is sort of boring."

"Nothing wrong with boring," said her father. "The other one though, the wog, I would stay away from him if I were you."

She didn't know what a wog was but it was obviously someone her father didn't approve of. He had his theories about people, was always comparing them to horses: workhorses, racehorses, show horses.

"You are a thoroughbred," he told her once. "Not like other people. Don't ever forget it."

When no one was around she pulled the dusty dictionary off the living room shelf and looked up "wog." The definitions made little sense because, though Ian had dark hair, he was neither a native of the Middle East or Africa nor a black-faced doll, nor was he a "small insect; a germ or organism causing infection; an illness or disease."

She wasn't going to ask her father what he thought a wog was. She wasn't going to ask anyone about Ian because they might guess what she felt. She only knew that he was at least four years older than she and that his father had some sort of business connection with Tom's father, who was Mr. Brooke's brother. And he was the most perfect male person she had ever seen. Better even than her father.

CHAPTER 3

BURNMOUTH

If you can think of life, for a moment, as a large house with a nursery, living and dining rooms, bedrooms, study, and so forth, all unfamiliar and bright, the chapters which follow are, in a way, like looking through the windows of this house. Certain occupants will be glimpsed only briefly. Visitors come and go. At some windows you may wish to stay longer, but alas. As with any house, all within cannot be seen.
James Salter, *Burning the Days*

For as long as any of them could remember Katie and the other grandchildren felt Burnmouth was their kingdom, and Granny McAllister their dowager queen. They couldn't have been happier subjects.

Katie and her eight cousins thought Burnmouth was perfect.

There were lily-of-the-valley-sprinkled woods to hide in, the great sloping lawn to roll down like a sausage, the enormous oak tree to swing from, the vegetable garden to pull up radishes and carrots, the formal garden to pick bouquets for play weddings, and the beach where the cousins established their Pretend City. Enclosing them away from the Real World was a long gravel driveway with twists and curves and a bridge over the brook that gave Burnmouth its name. When tennis, swimming, and sailing lessons weren't interrupting, the children were turned loose to roam this kingdom and do whatever they wanted.

Sometimes Katie undertook her own private expeditions beyond the boundaries. The children weren't allowed to cross Eden Street, where tourists' cars whizzed by on their way into town, but Katie, very carefully, did anyway. She ducked under a rusty chain across an overgrown driveway that led to a deserted forest. Not far in, there was a tree-stump castle on a floor soft with pine needles and moss, under a canopy of ancient branches. She could see only jagged pieces of sky far above her, and she could barely hear the swishing of the cars. There was no one around anywhere. Out of scale to her miniature castle, she felt like a goddess. She returned here whenever she wanted to be alone, and never told the others that such a place existed.

Every summer morning, beginning when she was very little, Katie climbed into bed with her grandmother and cuddled. She hoped she would never be as fat as her grandmother, who was draped in soft skin and silky nightclothes, but she loved that Granny McAllister was majestic, a mountain of dependability and order. Queen Victoria. The Old Lady Who Lived in a Shoe. An enormous cream puff.

"How's my girl?" Granny always giggled, putting aside the breakfast tray, opening the covers so she could crawl in. Katie played with the diamond bracelet, spinning it around the mottled wrist above the striated nails, the nails that Katie had been allowed to paint since she was eight. The tan polish was called "Windsor."

"Gramama Lewis gave me this bracelet when I married, and I'll give it to you when you get married," she told Katie. "Of course if I die first you'll have it then."

Then Granny would giggle some more and cough a bit because she smoked. "I'm not sure if they'll be able to get it off. I've gotten so fat!"

Granny's hearing aids were on the bedside table so Katie yelled at her:

"Don't die first, you have to be at my wedding. I want my wedding to be in this house and you have to be here."

Katie was already practicing walking down the stairs that fanned out from the curved wall like a huge shell, imagining how she would throw her bouquet from the top, careful not to clobber the chandelier.

Each morning the cook would come in and stand resolutely in her white uniform with a little pad while she and Granny discussed what to have for dinner and what to order from Butterfield's. Behind them Agnes laid out Granny's clothes on the chaise longue: the long stockings, the girdle, whichever wool suit (for it was almost always chilly in the summer) and blouse Granny decided on. Agnes placed the big white shoes side by side on the floor.

Then Katie would be shooed away while Agnes helped Granny dress.

"The Instigator," the grown-ups called Katie. As the oldest of nine cousins, she shepherded the other children, organized their adventures, led them into temptation.

Katie bid the cousins tiptoe up the creaky back stairs to the forbidden third floor where the maids lived. Here in a hot, dusty attic they plundered the costume trunk. They struggled into velvet vests, ruffled petticoats, a Beefeater jacket, drummer boy uniforms, gypsy shawls, feathered hats like in Puss n' Boots. "I get to wear Grandpa's sweater," several kids demanded every time. The sweater had "Yale 1900" actually knitted in, not stuck on top. Nobody knew why Granny had divorced her husband, but because Granny was perfect the children assumed Grandpa did something terrible. That made his sweater even better.

Katie decreed that the cousins give weddings. The girls always wanted to marry Rex, as did little Sebastian, but Rex wanted to be the minister so he could make a speech. He was good at that sort of thing, being Uncle Oliver and Aunt Pru's son. He tied a linen napkin around his neck and tucked the corner into a black garment bag with holes cut in the bottom for feet. No one ever wanted to marry Katie, who was taller than the others, even when she got herself up prettily with the lace bureau scarf on her head and a real dahlia on top of that. Carrie, who always seemed a little left out, usually consented to be the groom, borrowing one of Uncle Peter's hats and the huge navy blazer from the front hall closet that some guest had forgotten years ago.

"Dearly beloveds, we are gathered here today to form a more perfect onion," intoned Rex. "We celebrate the alienations of generations of McAllisters, Bowmans, Burtons, and so forths. May God be with you."

"And with thy spit," said Fred, the next oldest boy. The marriages took place in the little sitting room with the silk curtains, and Agnes was not happy with the rice throwing that ensued. Out roared the enormous vacuum cleaner and chased them away.

Carrie was usually dragooned into being the patient when they played "Doctor" and she often got upset and had to be held down.

Once, on the maids' day off, they almost sent Sebastian down to the laundry room in the pantry dumbwaiter. The biggest boys had gotten him all folded up inside it, when Sebastian suddenly began to scream in terror. Katie lifted him out and held him until he stopped crying and forgot all about it, ready for the next adventure.

The most exciting summer event for the grown-ups was the Club costume party. The children buzzed around making nuisances of themselves trying to help. They were proud of their brilliant parents, aunts, and uncles, but wished they could go too.

"Come on," begged Katie, "Why can't we?"

"Mrs. van Linden took her grandchildren once," said Rex. There had been a picture in the *Ellsworth Times* of the famous mystery writer dressed as a squaw with a descending line of ten grandchildren in fringe, feathers, leather, and moccasins.

That Granny stood around looking worried and biting her lip made watching the preparations even more fun. She had never gotten over the time Zack went as a masseur pushing

Nancy in an old claw-footed bathtub on wheels, fake bubbles up to her bare shoulders. It looked as though Nancy was naked.

"I don't like it one bit," Granny had said.

"But Mother, everyone will know I've got on a bathing suit under the bubbles. And then after the grand march I'll change into my evening dress."

"I'll protect her honor," said Zack, spiffy and seductive in his high-necked white masseur's uniform, a big smile on his face. Even Granny couldn't resist Zack's charm most of the time.

Nancy and Zack won first prize that year and also the year of "Come as your Pet Aversion," when Nancy dressed as Zack and Zack dressed as Nancy. But Aunt Pru and Uncle Oliver won when the theme was "Favorite Songs." They went as "Passengers Will Please Refrain," the song about not flushing toilets in the train station set to the tune of Dvorak's *Humoresque*. A local carpenter made them an upright coffin-like box on wheels with a black curtain covering the open side. Uncle Oliver wore a porter's uniform and covered his face with black shoe polish. Inside, Pru sat on a toilet in her long flannel nightgown.

Later when he became a respected civil rights lawyer in Philadelphia, Uncle Oliver worried that someone might have seen the pictures.

The year of "Your Favorite Nursery Rhyme" Nancy and Zack went as The Owl and the Pussy-Cat. Zack had the local sign maker make a pea-green little boat with the first stanza of the poem printed on its sail. Getting the honey and the five-pound note was easy but Zack insisted on having a piggy-wig too. He took the bigger boys with him to the farm, and Rex got to carry the piglet into the front hall where the other children had gathered to welcome it. That's where it wiggled out of Rex's arms and skidded off on the polished floors toward the living room. Katie was sure Rex loosened his grip on purpose. They went running after it, chasing it around the furniture, under the antique tables, under the silk upholstered love seats, behind the heavy linen curtains, the older children laughing, the littler ones screaming, the piglet too terrified to make any noise at all. Agnes came bounding in from the pantry wielding a broom, and Higgins the gardener finally grabbed the squirming bundle and deposited it in an upstairs bathtub. Nancy and Zack won first prize that year.

In the old photograph in the living room an earlier Granny sat on a wicker bench in front of a painted wisp of a landscape. Granny, already old in her thirties, her great silk lap spread beneath her lacy bosom, her soft hair, said to have been a magnificent strawberry blond, in a knot behind her head, sat like a Leonardo da Vinci madonna with an earlier generation of children arranged around her.

The oldest, Vanessa, nicknamed Nancy, looked serious, adorable, a huge bow topping her ringlets. Prudence, age about two, in a white organdy dress and perfect little shoes, appeared already eager to live at a crazy angle to the world, determined to be more interesting than the perfect Nancy.

Peter Junior, the youngest, grinned like a happy kid. You'd never think he'd grow up to be an alcoholic and get kicked out of Yale. "Uncle Peter helped build the Cadillac Mountain road," some grown-up always announced proudly as Granny's old Packard labored up to the summit so the family could extol yet another sunset. (During the war the children loved it when Granny would turn off the engine in order to save gas and they coasted all the way down.)

Aunt Pru had grown up to marry Uncle Oliver, a rotund attorney with eyes that looked like pinholes inside thick glasses. Back in Philadelphia they maintained a messy house, embraced liberal causes and embarrassed their neighbors. Negroes and people in turbans came and went.

There was more information lurking in the scrapbooks in Granny's desk's bottom drawer, brittle tan pages flaking inside rough black covers. Newspaper clippings from around the First World War, parties in Chicago with Granny sad in long shapeless dresses. Mr. and Mrs. Peter McAllister were entertaining some Italian dignitaries. They were sailing on the Queen Mary. They were spending the winter in Cannes. They were summering in Maine. Mrs. McAllister and other ladies (all of whom wore black lipstick) were rolling bandages for the Red Cross. Peter McAllister, Esquire, was a "silk stocking alderman."

What on earth did that mean? Stories explaining how he lost his second election to a war hero were pasted in as well.

It was obvious her mother's family was better than her father's Boston family, who were descended from Puritans. Katie and her family lived in Boston and so she was subjected to the Bostonian aunts all winter long. They talked about health and the weather and they didn't give parties or drink. A glass or two of sherry on holidays, that was about it.

Those afternoon chamber concerts they took her to at the Gardiner Museum were almost enough to turn Katie off from culture forever.

Clearly the McAllisters were richer and more glamorous.

History books occasionally reminded the children of the religious upheavals that had brought their ancestors from England, but now religion provided only the faintest background music to their lives. "Gave his only begotten son," "Suffer the little children," "God of our fathers," and best of all, "Eternal father, strong to save, Whose arm hath bound the restless wave...." Lovely phrases suspended in the gloom of churches at Easter, weddings, christenings, and funerals, along with the sounds of organ music and rumbling stomachs, and the scents of lilacs, or peonies, or lilies.

Granny McAllister attended Chicago's Fourth Presbyterian Church in the winter and Saint Saviour's Episcopal Church in the summer, but she said little about either except to comment on the hats. But Katie, ever exploring, became intensely religious when she was twelve. It might have had to do with the books she investigated, specifically with George Bernard Shaw's *Saint Joan*. It might have had to do with approaching adolescence and the realization that she was a bad person. When her mother scolded her for being mean to Carrie, she sometimes said, "You can be very selfish sometimes, Katherine Bowman. Just like your father."

Most likely Katie's "conversion" also had to do with her friend Jean, who had become religious as well, and whose brother Ed was Katie's crush that summer. The girls attended catechism classes at Saint Saviour's so that they might be confirmed in pretty white dresses on Labor Day weekend. They went to church on Sundays and sometimes Rowdy, Ed and Jean's filthy springer spaniel, came padding down the aisle, tail wagging, and licked their profiles while they prayed.

The McAllisters may not have honored seriously the traditions of their assigned religions but they religiously honored their own traditions.

For instance, even at home the McAllisters always "changed for dinner," which was different from "dressing" for dinner. It just meant they put on something nicer than sweaty shorts or dungarees. First a nice hot bath. "Nothing," remarked Granny McAllister frequently, "like a nice hot bath." Then cocktails. "As soon as the sun has crossed the yardarm." Whatever that meant. If everyone was home, and if "it" was nice, all ages congregated in the brown wicker chairs with the faded linen cushions on the veranda. The veranda was hung with drooping fuchsia plants and overlooked the lawn, the beach, and the bay. "Isn't it a lovely evening," someone always said.

A child would grab the binoculars out of their worn leather case and still be trying to focus on Bald Rock when another would try to snatch them away. "My turn!" would begin a squabble soon ended by dirty looks from the parents and Granny biting her lip, a gesture that could paralyze the most brazen child.

Agnes would bring the cocktail things on a tray. "Somebody get the door for Agnes!" and a child would jump up and tug at the reluctant screen door that never came open all at once. On the tray were Old Fashioned glasses, bottles of bourbon, gin, and vermouth, and ice cubes in a silver bucket with little tongs. A bottle of bitters and a jar of that gooey orange stuff from S. S. Pierce. There was always a cocktail shaker. Every family they knew had a silver cocktail shaker with the signatures of the father's wedding ushers etched into it. How they ever managed to get those feathery signatures into the hard silver was another thing at which the children marveled. All different kinds of handwritings were represented, just like on the Declaration of Independence, which they were told included a couple of signatures made by great-great-great-great grandfathers. "The Signers" these people were called.

And so the family wove itself a chain of summer traditions studded with memorable events like picnics and parties—costume or otherwise—pretend weddings, child-written plays, and minor disasters like the clambake when Petey fell into the chowder (he wasn't really hurt but he screamed a lot). Eventually the chain, as though it were made of wildflowers, would wither and dry and turn into memories, memories that stayed with Kate and her cousins far into old age. Or as far into old age as each of them was able to get.

CHAPTER 4

THE BASEMENT PLAYROOM

Yes, books! Cicero and Ovid have told us that to literature only could they look for consolation in their banishment.... No young man should dare to neglect literature. At some period of his life he will surely need consolation.
Anthony Trollope, *The Duke's Children*

It had lately occurred to her that her mind was a good deal of a vagabond.
Henry James, *The Portrait of a Lady*

In the early '40s, as the nine McAllister grandchildren slowly woke into awareness of their lives, they knew "there was a war going on." They knew that people were bombing and shooting on the other side of the ocean and even children were getting hurt.

At Katie's school in Boston, when the fierce lady teachers weren't watching, the janitor played the "White Cliffs of Dover" on the upright piano and the little girls clustered around looking over each other's shoulders at the words, singing as best they could. It was the least they could do to help Jimmy "sleep in his own little room again."

Then the war was over and after the radio had been turned off, the church bells stopping ringing, the bonfire's embers cooled, and the tears of happiness wiped away, a new dark thread became woven into their happy summer days: The Atomic Bomb. Being the oldest Katie was perhaps more aware of this than the others. Sometimes out of nowhere when she was feeling particularly happy, she remembered how Daddy said someday the Atomic Bomb might blow up the whole world. When she was little she had been assured that the guns in France and England couldn't reach to the Ocean Drive, but this new thing could reach everywhere and nobody could do anything about. It lay there at the back of her mind like a sleeping snake.

Katie was the first of the cousins to reach puberty. As Katie became older, and then with puberty suddenly much older, she spent more time alone. By the time she was fifteen the shenanigans of the cousins seemed to be those of a different generation. And though people could not possibly guess by looking at her, Katie was busy developing a "rich inner life."

On days when the fog obliterated the world and Muggins, the mournful foghorn, reminded people they weren't welcome outdoors, the playroom was her perfect refuge. Burnmouth was built on a hill, so the damp and gloomy playroom was beneath the other rooms; a staircase under a broken cuckoo clock led down from a small sitting room. In this place where the silt of childhood summers accumulated, and grown-ups never ventured, Katie felt both separate and connected.

It was a place where bushes scratched never-washed windows, moisture softened never-cleaned upholstery, and the window seat's knobbed cushioning had long ago ceased to invite. At one end stood an ancient pool table on which the cousins played, taking into account its tilted topography. At the other was the old Victrola that you had to wind up. It sang World War I songs like "Pack Up Your Troubles in Your Old Kit Bag, and Smile, Smile, Smile." Another song told of how even young prunes have wrinkles.

There were a few wobbly iron lamps covered with dark orange shades, which excited various insects when Katie turned them on, and bookshelves everywhere.

The shelves housed hundreds of mildewing books that she felt had been waiting for her, waiting for decades to be read again. Opening them gave off a delicious odor that was both damp and dusty, and she went through them like a ravenous mouse. *The Princes in the Tower, The Man in the Iron Mask, A Tale of Two Cities, Captains Courageous, The Scarlet Pimpernel*, stories about King Arthur and Robin Hood. The diary of a Russian countess who knew the men who killed Rasputin entranced her.

But best of all was the story of Roger Bacon, the medieval friar who in his dingy laboratory constructed a human-like head of brass. He was determined the head would speak, and speaking, tell the secret of the future. Katie read over and over about the friar waiting night and day to hear the mechanical voice and, when he could no longer stay awake, the brass head thundering amidst smoke and fire, "Time was. Time is. Time—" and then exploding. Katie was fascinated by this ancient scholar who tried to break the rules of nature; she was fascinated by secrets.

Even at fifteen Katie ran up the playroom stairs as fast as she could so that no nameless something could snatch at the bottom of her sweater, but her heroes were afraid of nothing. Except for St. Joan, Cleopatra, Mata Hari, and the Little Colonel, she always identified with the men: the swashbuckling heroes, the explorers, and the survivors of terrible ordeals and dangerous voyages. She particularly admired spies. She was disappointed to learn that Mata Hari, in her jewel-encrusted bra, and the Little Colonel, in her uniform, worked for the wrong side in the Great War; she wondered if it was still all right to admire them.

Having carried Shaw's plays to her bedroom for privacy and better light, she became Cleopatra, "the sacred cat of Egypt," or Joan of Arc, stomping around declaiming: "They told me you were fools and would make me drag about in a skirt!"

Books created an alternative life, and when she felt hurt or lonely, this life constructed of words was a place she could escape to, a place where her sad self disappeared and she lived the lives of others.

In costumes and books and make-believe Katie dreamed of her grown-up life, and she dreamed literally. On the border of sleep, she would travel the world, visiting places she had never seen, castles and valleys, mountains, medieval towns, Arabian cities, and vast deserts. On waking she would try to continue the dreams' narratives, nudging their nonsense into stories of handsome men who saved her from disasters.

She herself was a spy, a superwoman, a brave explorer, and only a man even more super than she was could win her heart. And now at fifteen, she knew what he looked like. He had dark hair, fine features, deep eyes. He looked like Ian.

Sometimes a dream would emit an aura that would continue throughout the day and beyond; some of these auras stayed with her for years. So perhaps it was inevitable that she would be hit hard by love.

Chapter 5

MRS. WHITE'S DINNER PARTY

"Oh, how wonderful to be your age!" said Anna, "I remember that mist, like the blue mist over the mountains in Switzerland. It covers everything when childhood is just ending, and out of that happy, care free time, out of that immense merry circle, a path begins to develop that grows narrower and narrower."
Leo Tolstoy, *Anna Karenina*

If the great world of society were a university...the magna cum laude honors would be awarded...to her who knows best every component detail of preparation and service, no less every inexorable rule of etiquette, in formal dinner-giving.
Emily Post, *Etiquette*

Mrs. White said we don't have to dress for dinner," Nancy told Zack as she hung up the phone one day the summer Katie was fifteen. Some of the younger children laughed overhearing this. They knew that "dressing for dinner" meant white dinner jackets (in the summer) and long dresses, but they liked to imagine the grown-ups sitting around the table, fat and thin, old and young, men and women, eating dinner naked.

The morning of Mrs. White's party, Nancy called to Katie, "Mrs. White is on the phone for you."

Why on earth would Mrs. Andover White, one of Granny's best friends, a really old lady, want to talk to Katie? Katie rolled her eyes and raised her eyebrows like Groucho Marx before taking the receiver. "Hello, Mrs. White," she said breathlessly.

"Katie, dear, I have an enormous favor to ask of you," said the croaky but elegant voice. "Mrs. Patterson has come down with the flu and you know how dreary it is to have too many extra gentlemen at the table."

"Oh," said Katie who thought there could never be too many extra gentlemen anywhere. "Of course."

"So, though I realize it's the last minute, I was hoping you would join us for dinner tonight."

"Oh," said Katie again, thinking of her movie date with Michael Blake. "I'd love to. Thank you so much."

"Don't bother to dress," said Mrs. White.

Later when Katie was getting ready for the party Nancy knocked on her bedroom door.

Katie, who was in her underwear, opened the door a crack.

"A word to the wise," said Nancy. "Not the black dress."

"Okay," said Katie, disappointed. But this party was after all the grown-ups' world, and later she was happy when everyone said she looked lovely in the pink sundress with the white cardigan over her shoulders, red Capezio ballet slippers on her feet.

There was no one else there under forty.

As they wandered in from cocktails Katie almost gasped at the beauty of Mrs. White's dining room table. In the center lilies, roses, hydrangeas, baby's breath, and other white flowers cascaded from an intricate vase. The place mats were lacy, too, as were the edges of the monogrammed napkins. Ivory candles in crystal candelabras made the mahogany table and its silverware gleam. Little families of stemmed glasses rimmed with gold were clustered beside place cards written in a shaky hand; yellow and lavender pansies floated in finger bowls.

Katie hoped she would use the right fork.

The publisher who had almost swallowed her earring at the Club dance pulled her chair out for her and then stood at his place until all the ladies had been seated. Mr. Brooke sat on her right.

"Well, my pretty one," said the publisher, dipping the tips of his long fingers into his finger bowl, wiping them daintily on the huge napkin, and deftly removing the doily and bowl without disturbing the equilibrium of the floating flower, "tell us your plans for the future." The silk ascot at his neck was even more beautiful than the last one.

The future? David Brooke jumped into her hesitation.

"She'll marry someone rich and famous. With looks like Katie's she'll rise to the top, find herself a senator or a diplomat. Of course I'd prefer to snag her for my nephew Tom, but poor Tom...."

"Of course, she will have any man she wants," interrupted the publisher, "but I would hope she'd have a brilliant career herself. Reportage, perhaps?"

"I'd love to be a report—" began Katie.

"Nonsense," said Mr. Brooke, "that would be a waste of her talents. I can see Katie in a grand house, or two or three grand houses, possibly one in France, and Barbados, with a retinue of faithful servants, some racehorses to play with..."

"And on the cover of *Town and Country* more than once," said the publisher scornfully, turning to the lady on his left as he gave Katie's knee a little squeeze under the table.

Katie tried to be interested in Mr. Brooke, while noticing the parents of Carrie's first boyfriend at opposite ends across the table. She shuddered to remember how their only son had drowned the summer before and fourteen days later, his body, as predicted, had washed up on a neighbor's beach. Carrie, naturally, had been devastated. They all were, horrible things like that weren't supposed to happen in the summer. The grown-ups gossiped about the bereaved couple with a combination of affection, pity, and disdain; Katie knew that they had probably come in separate cars so that neither had to drive home with a drunk.

Katie tried to concentrate on the emerging discussion about whether townspeople (as opposed to the "natives" who were fishermen and servants) should be invited to join the Club.

"After all," said Mr. Brooke, "there are some very bright people over at the lab." (He meant the Jackson Laboratory, where they were doing things to mice to find a cure for cancer.)

"Bright, perhaps," said a lady, "but would they feel comfortable at our Saturday night dances?"

"Do you suppose they own dinner jackets?" asked another.

At dessert, Mrs. White made the men change places and now a naval officer in an elaborate white uniform took the seat that Mr. Brooke had vacated. There was a U.S. Navy ship in the harbor, as there often was in July, and this gentleman was apparently its captain.

"What are you doing with all these old folks?" he whispered to her.

"Learning about life," she answered with a hint of a giggle.

Feeling flushed and pretty, Katie was having a wonderful time at Mrs. White's dinner party. It wasn't only the "extra gentlemen" who paid attention to her, and she could see that not just Nancy, but Zack, too, looked proud.

Until then Katie had assumed that when dinner was over and the ladies and gentlemen retired to different rooms, the men with their cigars and their politics had more fun. How wrong she was!

After dinner the gentlemen, clapping each other on the backs, were off to the library, while the ladies followed Mrs. White into her ground floor boudoir for coffee and chocolates. It was a gentle little room, flowered chintz enhanced by ribbons and ruffles, the perfect setting for this bejeweled dowager. Winifred White, whose husband had invented the radio or the telegraph or something of that sort, was approaching her nineties. She carried her magnificent rump and bosom regally, all of it upholstered in satin as silvery as her upswept hair. In a circle around her the other ladies balanced demitasse cups on their nylon knees as gracefully as they could. Tiny silver spoons danced in china saucers as the ladies tried not to laugh too hard at the gossipy delights spilling out of the old lady. The fact that young Katie was among her audience didn't for a minute cause Mrs. White to censor herself; it might even have inspired her.

After a string of comments as witty as Cole Porter lyrics, Mrs. White settled her sparkling spectacles on Katie. "Well, Katie, my dear," she said, causing eight pairs of female eyes (including Nancy's) to turn on the fifteen-year-old. "Tell us about young Tommy Brooke and that very attractive tutor of his. I hear you had a lovely time with them at the movies the other night."

Blushing Katie, determined to survive the inquiry with grace and wit, was disappointed when Mrs. White submerged her only briefly in embarrassment before fishing her out again.

"No, no, no, I don't want you to betray your friends by subjecting them to nosy old ladies such as myself. I imagine poor Thomas's mother running off with a Catholic priest was a bit upsetting for him."

Then, turning to the others, she went on:

"Though I understand what a tonic a bit of papism must have been for poor Mary Ann after years of marriage to that boring puritan. Besides, I've heard priests can be delightful in bed."

"Imagine finding one's way through all those black clothes," suggested another lady of Mrs. White's vintage.

"Undoing that turned-around collar, I suppose one would start there," said someone else.

"Oh, I don't know," said Margaret Louise van Linden, causing a sputtering of little laughs. "I think I might leave that on till last!"

"They say nuns' habits are considered very sensual by some men," offered yet another, "so perhaps the reverse is true."

Katie thought this would be quite all right with her, a life like this, surrounded by ladies like these.

Then her mother changed the subject. She was after all the only one there with a fifteen-year-old daughter in tow.

"I understand Tom Brooke is being tutored in math this summer. Such a difficult subject for many people." (Though not for her mother, thought Katie. Nancy, like Ian, was a whiz at math.)

"Thank goodness those days are over," said Margaret Louise van Linden. "Though if I had a tutor as good looking as that one I might take it up again."

"Tell us about your new book, Margaret Louise," persisted Nancy.

CHAPTER 6

GOLDENROD

The summer evening had begun to fold the world in its mysterious embrace. Far away in the west the sun was setting and the last glow of all too fleeting day lingered lovingly on sea and strand. James Joyce, *Ulysses*

I adore goldenrod," Nancy said one day in mid-August. "But still, I hate it when you start to see it at the side of the road. I hate what it means."

Kate, disconsolate that she had only really seen Ian at a distance this summer, began counting the days until everyone would return to the Real World. In less than three weeks Granny would go back to Chicago, as would Uncle Peter and his new wife, and Sebastian and his brothers and sister. Aunt Pru, Uncle Oliver, and Cousins Rex, Fred, and Martha would go back to Philadelphia, and the Bowmans back to their Boston suburb. After Labor Day Burnmouth would be boarded up again for the winter, the furniture covered with muslin and the water drained from the pipes.

On a dreary Sunday afternoon Zack Bowman stood at the long living room windows and stared out at the gray sky and the bay, its water heaving sullenly like molten lead.

"The weather's very anthropomorphic," he said and Katie, though she wouldn't admit it, knew exactly what he meant. Her own moods seemed at the mercy of the weather.

"What did he say, Nancy?" asked Granny.

"He said the weather is very anthropomorphic."

"Goodness, what a big word," said Granny.

Perhaps boring Sunday afternoons were God's punishment for their not going to church, thought Katie, though by this time she was not so sure about God. Lunch with its rare roast beef, gobs of gravy, and yellow Yorkshire pudding, followed

40

by chocolate sauce slithering over vanilla ice cream, kept the gloom away only temporarily. After they had scraped back their chairs and Agnes began to clear the table, the children followed slowly as Granny toddled toward the living room on Uncle Peter's arm. Next Granny distributed the candies from Miss Lufkin's, which the children knew Granny hid in the second tiny drawer to the left in the upper middle of her desk, but which they never stole. After that some of the children crowded around the card table in front of the fireplace, and worked at the jigsaw puzzle. The thatched-roof cottage was becoming surrounded by a rose garden but completion was a long way off. Every now and then Nancy looked up from her needlepoint and with a deft movement of her capable fingers inserted a perfectly fitting piece.

"Why do you say the weather is anthropomorphic?" challenged Pru, looking up from the astrology column in the Bangor Sunday paper. Pru, being in touch with forces that controlled the weather, took it as an insult when people complained.

Her husband, Oliver, had appropriated the rest of the paper except for the comics, which the children had left scattered on the floor. Granny, her ritual duties completed, rummaged for her knitting in a floppy bag with wooden handles and Uncle Peter was trying to get his pipe started.

"Those clouds and I are equally dreary," Zack explained.

"And if the sun were out would you and the sky be equally blue?" asked Rex, who was considered the cleverest of the children.

"If the sun were out I would feel bright and sunny," said Zack. "And if the wind would die down I would feel peaceful and benevolent."

"And if it was raining you would cry," said Martha, who was ten.

"Maybe we should ask Agnes to light a fire," said Granny.

"Why don't you curl up with a good detective novel," suggested Nancy, who loved Dorothy Sayers.

"I hate detective novels. I think I'll go for a drive."

He left the room without inviting anyone to join him, and Nancy wondered which of his young blondes he was intending to visit.

That spring at her annual appointment, their family doctor had asked Nancy why she didn't divorce Zack. All those infidelities.

"Because no one ever invites a single lady anywhere," Nancy told the doctor, "and besides, he's good company."

Later she felt what a frivolous thing it had been to say; Dr. Kurland must have thought her daft. She had long had a crush, as Katie would say, on the handsome doctor and lying there naked except for one of those awful gowns always made her feel off her game. Still it was true, staying married to Zachary Bowman was probably a lot easier than the messiness of a divorce. And somewhere deep in her bones she knew she loved him.

So now Nancy stopped herself from speculating further about either man and tried to concentrate on her needlepoint. She told herself yet again (as she had told Katie, who had recently asked about Daddy's girlfriends), "There's safety in numbers." She turned back to her silk-threaded needle, which would produce a golden lion on a teal cushion long before the children would have finished their cardboard cottage. In fact the jigsaw puzzle, if it were like its predecessors, would never be completed, the last pieces lost and the card table showing through like the Great Lakes on a map of the USA.

"Let's give a party," said Katie to Carrie. "I need something to look forward to."

She wanted to see Ian again. She had fretted throughout the weeks since their movie date because he hadn't paid attention to her, had only said hello as they passed at the Club, hadn't ever cut in on her at the weekly dances. She had tried to convince herself that he thought she was too young, which she was, but other boys paid attention and even Mummy and Daddy's men friends seemed to find her attractive. For instance her dinner partners at Mrs. White's, and the publisher who had taken her earring in his mouth.

She and Carrie liked giving parties together, preferably ones with mostly boys. Boys and a love of licorice gumdrops were practically the only things the sisters had in common. As though echoing Nancy and Pru, there seemed to be a built-in dichotomy between them. Or perhaps they were frightened of being compared and so acted as differently from each other as possible. Carrie was better at sports and excelled at lessons. She played tennis fiercely and could swim lap after lap without getting tired. She never daydreamed. She had probably already finished her school summer reading list while Katie was sampling the ancient books in the playroom. Katie was more artistic and more of a scatterbrain.

"You're so like your father," her mother often said affectionately, but Katie wondered if it were an insult.

Carrie was pale, Katie was dark. At Christmas Carrie got blue or green sweaters and scarves, Katie pink or red. Katie had asked her father why blond hair was better and he had answered, "Because of the way it catches the light." Carrie had the chiseled look of the McAllisters, a cool sort of beauty, while Katie had the more gypsy appearance of the Bowmans: disheveled dark curls, pink cheeks, a sensual mouth, and deep brown eyes.

"Onion soup dip and potato chips," said Carrie, her freckled nose squinching in delight.

"Candles in Chianti bottles," said Katie.

"People can wear blue jeans," said Carrie.

"But they don't have to," said Katie thinking of the black dress. Had Mrs. Higgins washed and ironed it?

"Let's make a list of who to ask," said Carrie and the two girls abandoned the jigsaw puzzle and went to sit on the window ledge where the others couldn't hear them. It was the wide ledge against which the McAllister couples posed for their joyless wedding pictures, peonies in huge vases behind them.

When the list contained more than a dozen names Katie said, "I'll go and start calling people."

She didn't want Carrie to listen so she went off to the telephone closet before her sister had a chance to follow. She stepped up into the little room off the front hall and closed the door. It was a tiny space against which no one ever closed the door and she felt nearly smothered by the raincoats, hats, and umbrellas heaped on hooks, the smell of the yellow foul-weather gear usurping the air. Burnmouth's only downstairs telephone was mounted on the wall, its bell-shaped receiver dangling beside it. While Katie waited for the operator's voice she contemplated the wall where decades of McAllisters had measured their growing children and some of their dogs. The penciled names and dates began about a foot and a half from the floor. First a few favorite dogs: the Bowmans' boxers Brutus and Angelica, who were still in residence, then dear old Humphreyetta, the Philadelphia Saint Bernard, then the human toddlers. The smudged names laddered up to where Uncle Peter's topped them all.

Katie found her own markings, beginning when she was still called Katherine, the last one two years ago when she had stopped growing. Then the operator was ready for her.

"726, please," Katie said, having memorized it.

Tom was off somewhere and Ian was put on instead.

"A party," said Katie, stumbling. "My sister and I are giving a party next Wednesday and we—"

"Sorry, who is this?"

"Oh sorry. Katie. Katie Bowman, you know, who you went to the movies with a few weeks ago."

"Katie, of course. In the beautiful black dress."

"With mud on it," said Katie in spite of herself.

"With mud on it. Very fetching," said Ian.

She imagined him smiling. He wasn't being mean, she decided. "How did you get mud on it?"

"My friend and me, we climbed up to where they're building the new ferry dock. The ferry to Nova Scotia."

"Oh, yes," he said. "I've heard about it. I'm from Montreal."

"Really?" said Katie. She had little idea about Montreal but she assumed it was exotic. And wasn't it French? Maybe that explained his looks and his manner. "I've never been to Montreal. Or anywhere in Canada."

"You will love it. A very exciting city. Lovely old buildings, lots of history. Maybe I'll take you there someday."

Katie didn't know what to say, but closeted among the coats she trembled.

They'd love to come to her party. Would it be all right if he brought his guitar?

The party began in the late afternoon on one of those days that seem poignantly short, too short to be part of the lingering summer. In the pink and blue sky seagulls screamed their complaints against the dying light. The basement playroom, this nearly subterranean repository of long-ago McAllister childhoods, was a true *wunderkammer*, and the sons and daughters of the Summer Colony investigated its curiosities until, needing fresh air, they propped the doors open with an encyclopedia and wandered out onto the grass.

Each teenager grabbed a beer or a Coke from the big tub, Katie carried out the bowl of potato chips, and Carrie the onion-soup dip. Katie, who had decided not to wear the black dress, was glad she could sit on the ground without worrying about mud. She wore jeans and her favorite pink Brooks Brothers button-down shirt. She had decided to leave the third button from the top undone.

Michael Blake plopped himself down next to her.

"You off to school soon?"

"In about a month. Too soon."

"I forget where it is."

"Outside Philadelphia."

"The Main Line?"

"Bryn Mawr. Bryn Mawr College is across the street and we get to go to their lectures and stuff."

"That's not far from us. If I'm home you can come to Sunday lunch sometimes."

"When does yours start?"

"In three weeks. Two more years. God, I'll be glad when I get out of there."

Katie had not gone away to school before. She looked forward to it with mixed feelings. A new adventure. A chance to get away from her parents' squabbling over who was going to pay Daddy's bills. But still, locked up with only girls for nine months for three years, she didn't relish that.

Her mother had gone to a boarding school in Virginia with horses.

"No horses for you," said Nancy when they were looking over the brochures. "I just hated all that riding, and all those girls who could think of nothing else!" A horse had apparently thrown Nancy once, "Right through the barn door."

"Maybe he knew you weren't a landlubber," Katie had laughed. She had no use for horses either, and so they had picked this nice school that had been started by Quakers and had an excellent academic reputation.

Katie looked around. Where was Ian? Oh, please don't let him be off somewhere with Jo. She always worried about Jo around the boys that she liked. Jo was very attractive, so calm and confident and never flustered at parties, or anywhere, really. Was it because Jo's parents were so rich and secure, not anxious about money the way Katie's were? Jo's father owned the Pennsylvania Railroad or something like that, while Katie's father never had a real job, was just always trying different careers.

"I'd better get more chips," she said to Michael, who was trying to light a match with one hand without burning his thumb.

The playroom was dark and gloomy as usual. She could make out only one figure standing with his back to her reading a book. Approaching nervously, she peeked over Ian's shoulder.

"Oh my God!" she burst out.

"What's wrong?"

"No, nothing," she squeaked, "it's just that, that's my favorite book!"

"Friar Bacon's Brass Head. 'Time is, Time was, Time—'"

"And then the explosion!"

"Great stuff."

"It's so spooky. Those old guys hunched over weird experiments in dark old laboratories, cobwebs, mice running around. It's so, so..."

"So medieval."

"Yes, medieval."

"And romantic," he added and she shuddered a little.

"Do you like science?" he asked. He took the book to the lumpy couch. She sat down next to him. The pages gave off the smell that she loved.

"I like the idea of it, I mean people trying to find out about the stars and the planets and the elements, the universe and everything...." and then she stopped as she could hear her voice beginning to sound too dreamy.

He was smiling at her.

"I don't like measuring" she went on, more decisively. "In fact, I hate measuring. Like recipes, I can't ever follow recipes, or instructions of any kind actually...." (Why was she babbling on like this?)

"You've taken chemistry?"

"I used to throw the salts into the Bunsen burner to see what color flame they'd make. So beautiful, those reds, oranges, and wonderful blue."

"Maybe you would have preferred chemistry when it was still alchemy."

"Alchemy, oh, yes, I love the idea of trying to turn things into gold."

"You're quite a rebel, aren't you?"

"Well, yes, I guess." She wondered if she was a rebel. She would be one if he wanted her to be. She would be anything he wanted her to be. In awe of his poise, self-assurance, and good looks, she felt her own personality dissolve into admiration for his.

They sat for a moment in silence. They could hear the others laughing and yelling outside. Someone seemed to have started a touch football game. He smiled that smile again and took her hand and she thought she would die of happiness right then and nothing else would happen in her life that could ever make her so happy again.

How apt, she would remember later, that it was in the playroom, the playroom with all its moldy mystery and its generations of books full of heroes and heroines, that her own hero first seemed to notice her.

Some of the other kids came bursting in. He squeezed her hand before he let it go.

"Come on out, Ian," Tom yelled. "Give us a concert!"

Ian lowered himself and his guitar onto the grass and the others flung themselves down near him. He commanded their attention like an actor or a priest, his body seeming to possess an inherent music. Katie sat with her feet tucked under her folded knees and then decided on the "Little Mermaid" pose instead. As Ian bent his head down over the instrument he cradled it as tenderly as one would cradle a child. Or a lover.

The first songs were American musical show tunes, then Marlene Dietrich and Edith Piaf. Then as it grew darker he switched to ancient ones, wistful Irish and Scottish songs. They made a perfect sound track for the evening, and the teenagers, as if under a spell, didn't sing along, they just listened. Besides they didn't know the words.

I am a man upon the land,
I am a silkie in the sea,
And when I'm far frae every strand,
My home it is in Sule Skerry.

One of the boys snickered and Ian fixed him with a smile both haughty and understanding. Some of the other boys fidgeted and a couple of them lit cigarettes but the girls, particularly Katie, sat mesmerized. Ian sang on:

It shall come to pass on a summer's day,
When the sun shines hot on every stone,
That I shall take my little son,
And teach him for to swim the foam.

He strummed a little before he sang the last stanza, then he looked up from his fingers and winked at Katie.

And thou shalt marry a proud gunner,
and a very proud gunner I'm sure he'll be,
And the very first shot that e'er he shoots,
He'll kill both my young son and me.

CHAPTER 7

THE BELL BUOY

Youth and the sea. Glamour and the sea! The good, strong sea, the salt, bitter sea, that could whisper to you and roar at you and knock your breath out of you.
Joseph Conrad, *Youth*

With the end of August in sight, Katie hoped to carve out a miniature summer from the days that were left, one stuffed with fun and excitement. And she was able to do this because after the party Tom and Ian seemed to want to see a lot of her. They sailed, they climbed mountains, they sat around the Club pool and the two boys danced with her at the Saturday night dances. Ian held her tighter than other boys did and sometimes sang the words softly into her ear, and sometimes she would stumble even though he was an excellent dancer and she never stumbled with anyone else. They used to joke in those days about boys getting erections when they danced: "Is that a Coke bottle in your pocket?" Katie thought she could sometimes feel Ian's Coke bottle.

One windy day Tom, Ian, Katie, and Katie's friend Jo took Mr. Brooke's sailboat way out into Frenchman's Bay.

"Let's try to tip it over," Tom suggested.

"Yes, let's!" agreed Katie. "We'll all sit to leeward and sail as close to the wind as we can!"

"Come on, you idiots!" said Jo. "This is not a good idea."

"It's impossible to capsize a Luders," said Katie. "I know, I've sailed with Mummy on really rough days!"

"What do you think, Ian, my friend?" asked Tom, a smirk on his face. It was a dare.

"I'm willing to see what will happen," said Ian.

Jo braced herself on the high windward side, and Ian looked amused, while Tom and Katie pretended to revel in water splashing over the rail as they skimmed the waves, the hull on its side, the mast at a 45-degree angle. A bell buoy's clanging became louder and louder and soon the great iron contraption loomed over them.

They sailed close to it and then came about, the sails seeming to explode when the wind snatched them.

"It looks like a huge dreidel," said Ian.

Katie had no idea what a dreidel was.

"Let's get off on it!" shouted Tom over the clanging and swishing and howling. "Come on Katie, let's see what it's like to ride a bucking bell buoy in the middle of the ocean!"

The sails flapped furiously as Tom gave the tiller to Ian and then leaped off and reached to Katie, who leaped after him as the boat bounced. The boat sliced away and Katie and Tom each clung to a leg of the cradle that held the giant bell, each with one foot tight against a support.

Katie—thrilled, scared, wet, freezing—was deafened by the clanging. She hoped that Ian could sail well enough to come back for them without wrecking the boat and dumping them all in the bay. One could survive only fifteen minutes in that famously cold water. But Ian seemed to know what he was doing because soon the boat tacked with little fuss and headed toward them. Tom jumped onto its stern and yelled, "Wait, we'll be back!"

Deserted on the buoy, Kate watched the boat sail away in order to tack again. It was only seconds but long enough for her to enjoy the power of her courage, her daredevil teenage courage. Alone on the unforgiving ocean, trapped inside a tossing cathedral, its bell calling seagulls to prayer, she became a part of the wind and the water. Then the boat tacked and headed back. She saw that Ian had climbed to the bow, where he stood next to the collapsed jib holding on to the mast with one hand.

"Jump! I've got you!"

He was balancing now, both his arms outstretched to catch her. She jumped from one pitching surface to the other, and felt him pull her against him. Her heart beat so hard she felt it would knock them both overboard.

"You crazy kid, you're freezing!" He bundled her into the cockpit, took off his windbreaker and sweater and wrapped them around her. Her nose was running, her wet hair was in her eyes, she burrowed her face into his shoulder while he hugged her and rubbed her back and shoulders. Her heart was still beating wildly even after her shivering subsided and all she could think of was that he was holding her tight in his arms at last. Her whole body ached in places it never had ached before and there seemed to be no more ocean, no more sky, no more boat nor other people, just Ian.

"Wow," she heard Jo's voice. "That was quite something. You two should be in the circus."

She wondered afterward if she would have done such a reckless thing if Ian hadn't been there. But she was glad that she had. She never forgot riding the bucking iron monster; years later she could still see the rivulets of ocean streaming over her topsider sneakers on the metal floor before her hero came to rescue her.

But in spite of their various summer adventures Katie never saw Ian alone, and his affectionate aloofness, his apparent decision that she should be Tom's girl and he just a brotherly companion, only made her want him more. And made her want something that she had hardly dared think about before.

CHAPTER 8

K-K-K-KATIE

I went to the animal fair,
The birds and the beasts were there.
The old baboon by the light of the moon
Was combing his auburn hair.
The monkey he got drunk
And sat on the elephant's trunk.
The elephant sneezed and fell to his knees
And that was the end of the monk, monk, monk.
Traditional Children's Song

Apparently Ian had done a good job of tutoring Tom because Tom got into Harvard and Ian didn't come to Maine the next summer, the summer Katie was sixteen. Nor did he come the summer she was seventeen. Katie had to make do with the regular boys she had known for years, and any of the houseguests or tutors that might be attached, and she tried to convince herself that they were equally suitable companions as they went about their summer nonsense.

Katie and her friends drank enormous quantities of beer and smoked and danced and necked and sailed; some played tennis and golf. Katie decided to give up all her lessons except for sailing; no more swimming laps unless she felt like it, and, though it annoyed her father, no more pounding across tennis courts with his voice yelling in her ear—whether he was actually there or not—"Keep your eye on the ball, damnit!" Of all the necessary accomplishments for a woman, Zack put tennis high on his list.

Katie and her friends looted the ruins of mansions that had burned four years earlier in the Great Fire, and carried off charred fixtures no one seemed to want: old-fashioned telephones, wooden toilet seats, and, once, a bathtub.

Katie's boyfriends thought an antique bathtub from the Hillsbury Mansion would make a nice thank-you present for Mrs. Bowman and Mrs. McAllister. Those ladies had been so understanding and kind, inviting them to family picnics and other excursions, letting them sleep in the playroom overnight when they were too drunk to drive home. So the boys carried off the ancient claw-footed tub and deposited it on the grass circle in front of Granny's house with a nice note attached to it. They should have known Granny would not be amused. She was even less amused when a huge sign saying "EAT AT KATE'S, CLAMS and LOBSTERS" showed up one morning propped up at the driveway entrance. Nancy threatened to call the police if it wasn't gone within the hour.

Katie and her friends went to dances twice a week at the Club, and on Saturday they wore black tie. "K-K-Katie" thumped the band when she appeared in the doorway blushing and expectant, her Capezio ballet shoes already tapping to the rhythm. Katie had become more and more popular until now Michael Blake, who insisted on wearing sneakers with his tuxedo, used a huge stopwatch to time how long each of his rivals could dance with her. A young bartender, an English divinity student with a summer job, sometimes traded his white and green uniform jacket with one of the boys so he could cut in on Katie. If Ian could only see her now, the belle of the ball!

Zack Bowman looked up and observed his little girl from the sidelines with a mixture of pride and jealousy. Then he put his arm around whichever young lovely on whom he was trying to concentrate, and swirled her out into the bobbing throng on the dance floor. "When I'm not Near the Girl I Love, I Love the Girl I'm Near." Katie knew this was his favorite song.

Once one of Katie's boyfriends hissed in her ear, "Your father is necking with Terry Strayfield in the card room." Katie ignored him.

Who would buy the band for another hour? People grew anxious as midnight approached; some of the boys checked their wristwatches as the girls leaned on their arms to peek.

Mrs. Tobin was always the best bet. Seemingly oblivious to everything, she sat only inches from the musicians on a little gold chair, and when the fat drummer burst into his solo she stuck out a dainty foot so he could tap the sole of her satin shoe. All the while her eyes sank deeper and deeper into her pudgy face.

Then, a few moments after midnight, for certainly no one was ready to go home, out would come Mrs. Tobin's checkbook from the beaded evening bag and all would be well.

"Oh, when the saints, come marching in!" Conga lines formed and the laughing people spilled down the steps, out onto the dark lawn splattered with lighted rectangles from the windows. Some more coordinated than others, they followed the band onto the flagstones and marched around the pool. Tuxedoed boys climbed up the tall diving platform and threw themselves into the water.

Once one of Katie's girlfriends actually dove off the top diving board. The others squealed and cheered and held their drinks high as the figure in fluttering evening dress came tumbling through the night and disappeared in a huge splash.

Katie envied this pretty dark-haired girl for being even more of a daredevil than she was; she never could have done that. She might, if tipsy enough, swim in evening clothes or even in underwear sometimes, surrounded by sparkling phosphorous, but she'd never fly through the air like that, suddenly nowhere at all, trusting to the gods of entertainment that she would land safely.

Certainly these adventures were not those of a typical American summer, as Katie would learn later. Later she would read that social historians lumped the setting of her childhood summers together with Newport and Murray Bay and other faded remnants of a gilded age. She would learn that money was the subliminal music playing under these charming scenes, sometimes loudly, sometimes softly. And that like oil or water or other necessities, money actually came from particular sources. Money was not just a natural thing that people were born with like the colors of their eyes, or the limits to how tall they would grow. Someday perhaps it wouldn't seem fair to her. But she was still a teenager, and during those beautiful summer months she didn't think about much of anything besides boys, and one in particular.

Though Katie kept hoping, there was no word, no sign of Ian; it was as though he'd never existed. And Katie certainly wasn't going to embarrass herself by asking anyone who might know. It was as though he was one of those silkie things he'd sung about and he had disappeared back into the sea, turned back into an aquatic creature who wanted no more to do with human beings.

CHAPTER 9

A CAMPAIGN

Boston hostesses of position have never failed to demand of those who remain on their lists, strict obedience to the tenets of ceremonies and dignified behavior; nor ceased themselves to cultivate something of the "grand manner" that should be the birthright of every thoroughbred lady and gentleman.
Emily Post, *Etiquette*

The great ballroom success, first and foremost dances well. Almost always she is lovely to look at....All things being more or less equal, the girl who dances best has the most partners. Let a daughter of Venus or the heiress of Midas dance badly, and she might better stay at home.
Emily Post, *Etiquette*

In Eleanor McAllister's day, and still in Nancy's, and even in Katie's, it was considered necessary that a young lady of a certain class be introduced to society upon graduating from secondary school. Since in the first half of the twentieth century many of these girls didn't go to college, some spent an entire year attending "coming-out parties," cotillions as well as luncheons, teas, tea dances, and "small" dances (the invitations always specified "small") given by relatives, friends, and friends of friends. Thus Nancy McAllister, smart as she was, and though she had been accepted by Bryn Mawr College, had followed her family's wishes and allowed this to serve as her "higher education."

Tradition decreed as well that each girl be presented at a cotillion in her own city, and then, depending on how rich and/or popular her family was, she was honored again at one or more private parties. On the East Coast the parties took place in June and in the summer, and then at Christmas they moved to Chicago and other cities. The point originally was for the girls to find husbands and for the young men to see what had become available in the way of future wives.

Katie, at the time, thought of herself as part of a new world and she wouldn't dream of not going to college. The school she attended outside Philadelphia had begun to open her eyes to new vistas; she had met girls who were not exactly like herself. How antiquated coming-out parties seemed. Katie didn't realize that she lived at the tail end of an old era, not at the beginning of a new one.

Though she had never come to know Ian well that one summer, nor had she seen him since, his smile continued to haunt her. Katie thought about Ian for the whole three years of boarding school and the intervening summers. Along with memories of sunny days and sparkling ocean, mixed with romantic ideas gleaned from old books, he had become such a familiar inhabitant of her imagination that she sometimes wondered if he really existed anywhere else.

Tom was one of the boys who took her out, but she never dared ask him about Ian. Any answer might feel like an electric shock. She dated others, too, but Ian had usurped her capacity for romance.

She looked forward to the coming-out parties as a distraction. And also as a challenge. If she couldn't have Ian she would be brutally popular at every party she went to. (And maybe, just maybe, Ian would be at one of them.) So when the time came she threw herself into the debutante season as into a military campaign. On the arm of her father, handsomer than ever in his white tie and tails, she giggled and blushed as he marched her the length of the Copley Plaza's gold and white ballroom to face the Boston dowagers. Zack didn't seem like a man who read a lot of history, but now he made her laugh by saying the militant ladies coming ever closer looked like the seventeenth-century clergymen Increase and Cotton Mather in drag. In spite of that she managed to execute her deep curtsy without stumbling, and the moment she'd worried about for years passed without disaster.

Across from the ballroom in those days was the Merry-Go-Round Bar. Katie went AWOL there for a while that evening listening to a couple of older college men tell risqué jokes when she should have been dancing. She even risked smoking in those unbelievably expensive long white kid gloves. Luckily someone tipped her off just in time that the terrible Miss X was on the prowl scouting for infractions. Miss X was the Boston manifestation of the fierce lady, usually of the single persuasion, who was hired to enforce each city's rules of gentility. If this discreet and genteel bouncer caught anyone "crashing" such a party for any reason or behaving otherwise badly (like drinking in a bar) she would remove the culprit's name from The List forever. The List contained the names of all boys and girls who would be invited to parties that year and probably for many years to come. So Katie scurried back into the immense ballroom flickering with music, mirrors, candlelight, and laughter, and was soon swirled away again.

Katie managed to remain on The List.

When she had exhausted the parties of Boston and its North Shore Kate decided to attack the parties on Philadelphia's Main Line by billeting herself with her friend Jo.

"Sure, come on down," said Jo. "Mother and Dad like you a lot; just don't try talking politics with them. And there are some really terrific parties coming up."

So she crashed many more parties, if you could call being brought along as someone's houseguest crashing. Running out of dresses, she sometimes commandeered Jo's, but also found she could disguise her own by adding big ribbon sashes of various colors.

Soon she had a reputation, though she wasn't sure for what (she remained relatively chaste), and no dearth of partners. If she ever danced with one boy long enough for her smile to tighten, or to run out of polite little questions ("Where did you go to school?" "What does your father do?" "What do you think about the atom bomb?" "Do you think we're all going to get blown up?"), she excused herself to go to the ladies' room. There she would wait out the next few dances until she guessed the young men were ready to appreciate her again. Being considered a wallflower was a defeat worse than death.

"God," said Jo. "You really are something. I mean everyone is talking about you."

"Really?" Katie was extremely pleased.

"Annie Davenport's brother told her some boys were discussing you in the men's room. They said was it possible for any girl to be as flaky as Katie Bowman. I'd take it as a compliment if I were you."

"Right, some compliment."

The parties were beautiful everywhere, tables covered with white, pink, or ecru linen around a dance floor, delicate gold chairs orbiting them, stemmed glasses circling glittering candelabras and flowers like constellations of jewels. The scents of roses, gardenias, and ladies' perfume and the cheerful thump of Broadway show tunes filled the summer air.

Boys bellowed and girls giggled while white-gloved waiters tipped bottles of vintage wines ("Red or white?" "What are we having?" "Both, please!") into the goblets of underage drinkers. Waiters inserted steaming silver platters of tiny lamb chops, minuscule cylinders of filet mignon, and medleys of baby vegetables between the chattering children. Every so often, when Katie twisted up to say "thank you," she would look into Hispanic eyes and wonder what thoughts they hid.

After dinner the waiters stood clutching linen-shrouded bottles, ready to spring into service should a guest tap his upheld glass. Between performing these little acts of mercy, the waiters watched slippers of gold, silver, or pastel silk fly across the parquet floor following bigger shiny black shoes. They saw pastel satin and tulle swish against black trousers; they saw smiling girls like Katie, with her bobbing curls, in the arms of a different partner every few minutes. Out of the corners of their eyes they took stock of the less fortunate girls whispering to each other at almost empty tables.

As in classical ballet, the boys and the girls dressed differently, played different roles; they looked forward to different destinies.

At their own tables, the grown-ups watched as well, caressing glasses less than half full of wine, liqueur, or scotch, appraising the scene under heavy lids.

"Whose daughter is that, the one with the pink cheeks and the sash to match?"

"Don't know. Maybe from out of town."

"I heard she's a McAllister granddaughter. You know, the Chicago McAllisters. Farm Machinery."

"Staying with the Gibsons, I believe."

"Of course. Josephine would know her in Maine."

"Quite something, isn't she?"

The grown-ups, finally bored with watching and gossiping, went off to bed, but the eligible young danced on, drank champagne until their teeth itched, talked and laughed until the band members packed up their instruments and the sky exchanged its stars for the dawn. Katie and some boys would often end up in the swimming pool, her "merry widow" underwear decent but suggestive, and her ruffled petticoats still lovely when wet and clinging to her legs. Like a soggy Moll Flanders.

There was no Ian at any of these parties. But maybe, she consoled herself, she would run into him next year. She had been accepted at Vassar, and Poughkeepsie wasn't so terribly far from Princeton.

CHAPTER 10

ZACK

The world is so big, so complicated, so replete with marvels and surprises that it takes years for most people to begin to notice that it is, also, irretrievably broken.
Michael Chabon, "The Film Worlds of Wes Anderson", *New York Review of Books*

A womanizing father, he's
The first life-threatening disease.
Frederick Seidel, "Love Song"

O ne of the season's prettiest debs is spending her summer vacation working in the sportswear department of R. H. White's," wrote the *Boston Herald*'s society editor. She didn't need to remind her readers that White's was no Bonwit Teller or Saks Fifth Avenue; they wouldn't be apt to run into Katherine Bowman selling skirts, shorts, and slacks to working-class women in a store where not much cost more than $2.99.

Katie was there because by the Fourth of July she had had enough of parties. She had decided to stay in Massachusetts and work at the musty old Boston department store instead. She and her father, who was trying out a new job at an ad agency, would live in the family's suburban house while the rest of the family was at Burnmouth. Maine could wait.

She looked forward to spending time with her father.

Katie had always been curious about him, and now that she was almost as old as those women he admired, she saw him differently. Maybe now their relationship would broaden and he would actually talk to her about the books he liked, the paintings he knew, the music he'd once loved to listen to. They would have a lot of time to talk.

When she was small they'd had so much fun together, singing songs, playing guessing games. She remembered it vaguely but happily. There was a photo of her in her high chair with Zack next to her and each of them smiling a super big smile, each of them holding a spoon with gunk on it, patting their chests and seeming to say, "Yum, yum, how delicious."

There were snapshots of the two of them when she was a two or three, staggering around blindfolded by napkins over their heads, in others they made faces as they pretended to be monsters.

Nancy had told her that as soon as Katie learned to walk Zack was always teaching her elegant little mannerisms: how to curtsy, how to "toe out" when she walked, how to say "how intwesting!"

"That's all you need, a kind of noise to make when men tell you something," Zack told the uncomprehending little girl more than once.

And Nancy would laugh because she knew exactly what he meant.

"They'll think you're a wonderful conversationalist."

Maybe Zack was one of the few men who hadn't wished for a son instead. Katie had always felt his delight in her.

But when she was eleven or twelve, and had become plump, he would poke at her middle and say, "What's this, an inner tube?" She wanted to die.

Now that she was pretty again and not fat she felt he appreciated her again, even though he couldn't make her play tennis. He had taught her to dance, though, or rather untaught her what the Boston dancing school they had both gone to had taught her, and they danced well together. They had even won a contest at the Club by dancing on a table. He was proud of her dancing.

In the seventeenth century, the Bowman family had made the mistake of landing at Hull on the coast of what would one day become Massachusetts and staying there to farm.

Not until much later did any of them stray as far as Boston. They farmed the rocky land at Hull, branched out to Cohasset and Hingham and stayed close to the sea. Some of the men became sea captains. Religious people, they built beautiful white-steepled churches and for generations attended them. Some contemporary members of the family bothered to trace their line back to England, but for all intents and purposes, starting out back in the middle of the seventeenth century on that unfriendly coast was beginning enough for an American family.

So they had missed a lot in the British Isles and the Continent, thought Katie later. They had missed the Enlightenment, and Napoleon, and the romantics, and all those revolutions. Except their own revolution of course. Katie wished they had stayed in England.

But certainly by the time Zack was born the family was steeped in culture. Some of the men had made it up to Harvard, and all of them read the Bible and Shakespeare and Hawthorne and Melville and romantic poetry and everything else they should have read.

Zack was the youngest after four sisters. His father (long dead) had been a boys' school headmaster on the South Shore, had gone to Harvard, and, it was said, could recite Dickens's *Christmas Carol* by heart. (Katie doubted that. Come on, every word?!)

The eldest sister was an accomplished violinist, and the family was proud that she had played solo with the Boston Symphony at least once. She knew Koussevitsky and Arthur Fiedler as well as prominent Unitarian clergymen. John Singer Sargent had sketched her portrait and she gave every member of the family copies of it. (Kate hung hers in the laundry room.) She had married a wool merchant, and until the wool business moved south, they had money for trips abroad in a Henry James sort of way. They lived in an Italian palazzo in Brookline with formal gardens and statues everywhere. Little Katie was once frighteningly reprimanded by her aunt for mixing two different scents of bubble bath in her tub, and this was the main memory she associated later with that house.

The second oldest sister was an accomplished pianist and painter of flowers and gentle landscapes. She might have been considered an American impressionist, what with the soft edges and lavender shadows. The third eldest had gone to Radcliffe at the beginning of the century, making her the intellectual of the family. The fourth was a great badminton player.

In stark contrast to everyone else in his family, who were almost religiously serious about high culture and proper behavior, Zack was the playboy.

Of course, with his dark curls, mischievous brown eyes, and easy laugh, Zack would have been the favorite, even if he hadn't been the only boy. And since his sisters and parents had always allowed him everything he wanted, and he was in his twenties in the 1920s, it's not surprising that he should have tried to lead a Scott Fitzgerald sort of life.

He had a nervous personality and a mind that tended to jump from one topic to the next. His attention spanned very short distances and stopped to contemplate a subject only if he thought it beautiful. Thus photography would have been a perfect occupation, if only there were a way to make money from it. Nevertheless, he spent as much time as possible photographing beautiful women, horses, seascapes, and parties. But aside from occasional spreads in *Town & Country* or other society magazines, he didn't make money from his pictures.

People said he was an "original," and it was true he seldom did things the way other people did. For instance, he made his breakfasts (in the winter, not at Granny's) by throwing everything in the Waring blender: raw eggs, toast, grape jelly, orange juice, butter, cream, sugar, and instant coffee. And then eating it. Yuck.

He was a wonderful tennis player and loved parties, dancing, and telling jokes. On the other hand Zack sometimes went to parties and fell asleep on the couch. Not because he was drunk—he was never drunk (he didn't drink more than a beer or two or occasionally a Planter's Punch)—but because he was bored. He once didn't like the boeuf stroganoff at a dinner party so he put the chunks of meat into his pocket-handkerchief. Later he sneezed, pulled out the handkerchief and the meat flew everywhere. Katie loved this story but was glad she hadn't been there.

Kate had a vivid memory of Zack wandering around the house (not Granny's house but the one in the winter) with nothing on but a large bath-towel and his fedora singing. "That old devil moon," and "When I'm not near the girl I love, I love the girl I'm near."

Boston's summer streets were hot and dusty. Their twists and turns trapped people in warm shadow as they hustled down the narrow sidewalks. Into this maze of commerce Zack dropped Katie off much too early every morning.

In the beginning Kate found it refreshing to be living this different kind of life, working like real people in the city, earning her own money. The first morning before the store opened, she perched at the counter of a nearby diner, drinking coffee and eating a jelly donut all alone, like a real career woman. Free and floating away from the world she'd always known, she felt powerful and optimistic.

In the evenings Katie and her father avoided returning to their messy house in the suburbs by going to movies. They did almost no housework. They "aired" the beds and "soaked" the dishes. They ate out almost every night, usually at the orange and blue Howard Johnson's that they both loved. Kate always ordered a hot dog in its cardboard cradle with miniature cubes of relish and Zack had double cheeseburgers. For dessert they had ice cream. Katie worked her way through nearly all twenty-eight flavors, but Zack invariably ordered the chocolate.

But getting him to talk wasn't easy. He had his head in the newspaper or was on the telephone, or off at the country club playing tennis. He didn't seem to pay much attention to her. But did he pay much attention to anyone? He was a great changer of subjects.

"So, Daddy...." she said one day as they drove into the city.

He must have known what was coming. Telling a joke was a way to set up a speed bump on the road to personal conversation.

"You know the one about the man who when it was time to pay for his lunch said to the proprietor, 'Hey, I never got a check?'"

"Oh, come on, Daddy, I've heard that one a million times."

Zack put on an old man's Jewish accent.

"'Don't need a check. Crumbs on the sleeve, that'll be a dollar for the bread; spot of gravy on necktie, the lamb stew, five dollars; milk on moustache, another buck; so the total seven dollars.' Then the customer let out an enormous burp."

"'Woops, I forgot the radishes!'" Katie and Zack exclaimed together.

"It's good to practice one's material," said Zack and they were both quiet after that.

But Katie kept hoping that their time commuting to and from work would let her probe her father's mysteries.

"Tell me how you met Mummy."

She'd heard her mother's side of the story. Nancy had come down for breakfast at Burnmouth one morning—it was soon after she came out—and there was Zack helping himself to scrambled eggs from the sideboard. Apparently he'd tagged along with some other houseguest. "I thought he was very good looking and I wished I'd had a better bathrobe on."

Now Katie heard Zack's version. "I met her at the parties one summer. I'd come up with Dave Brooke, I think it was. There was a big regatta, wonderful boats from everywhere in the harbor, and dances at night. Great fun."

"And when did you decide to marry her?"

Zack thought for a while. Katie wondered if he'd dare say again that he'd married her mother for her money.

"Well, not for a couple of years," said Zack as he maneuvered the car through the afternoon rush hour.

"What made you decide? What made you propose?"

"She was a great gal. Good looking in her way. Intelligent. Everyone liked her. Your grandmother was a little daunting but I figured I could win her over."

The traffic came to a stop and the honking began. Perhaps the cars all around them prompted Zack's next memory.

"Clarence Gooch was the town cab driver. I asked him one night on the way back from Burnmouth what he thought I should do."

"And, what did Mr. Gooch say?"

Zack lowered his voice and attempted a Maine accent. "Oh yes, sir, marry her by all means. Miss McAllister is a great lady. And from a good family."

One evening instead of Howard Johnson's they ate at the Ritz. Zack had mentioned that an old friend was coming up from Virginia to talk to him about a business proposition. Something to do with photographing horses.

"I would like you meet them," said Zack.

It turned out that this business partner was a lady of about thirty-five, maybe forty, and very beautiful. Her suit was the color of lime sherbet and seemed incapable of wrinkling, her pale leather heels were maybe snake or alligator skin, and she wore her blond hair in a not quite shoulder length pageboy. Her nails were pink. "I'm so happy to meet you, Katherine," she said in a soft southern accent, "Your father has told me so much about you." The word "father" had no *r* but an extra *h* in it.

The three of them perused their menus while sipping drinks in the high-ceilinged dining room. (Only Zack's menu had prices; Katie had peeked. She wondered how that was going to work out.) Katie remembered this room with its cobalt blue water glasses from when she was little and her grandmother sometimes stopped on the way to Maine and took them there, in the days when one went by train. The sisters always ate so much bread and crackers they were too stuffed to eat when the food came. Now Katie avoided the silver basket entirely as she watched Zack and the lovely lady from Virginia discussing horses and hunting and parties and people they knew in common. Sometimes the lady's voice was so low Katie couldn't overhear. Sometimes the lady put her pink nails on Zack's sleeve and Zack look handsomer and happier than she had ever seen him. Katie felt awkward and adolescent and said hardly a word.

"Well?" said Zack in the car as they drove home.

"Well what?"

"What did you think of her?"

"She's beautiful, of course. Why do you care what I think of her?"

"Because she's an old friend." He paused. "A very good friend."

Neither of them ever said any more on the subject. They never spoke of the pretty lady from Virginia again, but she had left an aura, like a perfume that never dissipates.

Katie liked the women she worked with selling sportswear. She liked the women she waited on. All of them were kind to her, and patient with her mistakes. They treated her as slightly exotic but non-threatening. They reminded her of Granny's household, except now she and they were on the same level. Perhaps that's one reason Zack and Katie began to squabble on the way to work.

"It's really not fair," Katie would say, the coming-out parties still fresh in her mind. "All that money that people we know have and other people barely able to get by."

"I take it you're espousing communism."

"No of course not." It was the days of Joe McCarthy and the blacklists. "But still you have to admit.... I mean, look at Granny's Household, and Agnes and everyone. They work so hard just so our family can give and go to parties and—"

The argument would usually include Zack saying something like the following:

"If there weren't great wealth you wouldn't have the Medicis and if you didn't have people like the Medicis you wouldn't have Great Art. No Michelangelo. No Sistine Chapel."

From the Medicis to Marx they found plenty to argue about, and Zack kept trotting out the thoroughbred analogy.

He did it every time Katie complained about her feet. The glamour of being a working girl had grown stale. "I'm so tired. They don't let you sit down ever except on your lunch hour. And the lunch 'hour' is only a half hour. Sometimes I hide in a dressing room and just collapse on the floor."

"What did you expect? You weren't bred for that kind of work, you're not a workhorse, you were bred for dressage."

Three years of the old bluestocking who taught history at boarding school and professed to be a socialist had gotten Katie thinking. Miss Wainwright had taught them about Marx, Sun Yat-Sen, and Kerensky. She hoped the girls would repeat to their parents the story of her wearing a red dress to the Russian Embassy reception. And Katie's friendships had branched out as well. There were girls from all over the world in her school. There were girls on scholarships. There were a few Jews and one Negro, whom Katie had once brought home for a night during a vacation. Nancy had been almost embarrassingly kind to her; Zack had stayed out of the way.

One morning on the way into the city Zack and Katie found themselves in a particularly explosive fight.

"You are so overbearing and difficult, you have to surround yourself with Yes Men. No wonder all your friends are Jews and Negroes."

Was it Needham or Newton or Brookline they were in? She wasn't sure, but she couldn't stand it anymore. The light was red so she pushed open the car door and dodged through traffic to an unfamiliar sidewalk. She stood there in her sandals in the heat and realized she hadn't grabbed her purse. She had no money, no identification, nothing. While she was wondering what to do next she heard honking behind her. The Volvo had circled around and come back. When they stopped at the next red light he reached over and kissed the side of her head. "Sorry," was all he said.

Katie began to cry. The tears were unstoppable, rolling down her cheeks, into her mouth, dropping into her lap, wrecking her eye make-up. She pulled down her side's visor and surveyed the wet, streaked face in its mirror. She gulped with misery, suddenly remembering how they sang songs as they drove between Boston to Maine every spring and fall. "Long ago and far away, I dreamed a dream one day...." And that one from the Hasty Pudding Show that she could never remember all the words to, "I want to go places and do things...." She was only a toddler when he first sang it to her.

"Come on, baby, cheer up. It's not the end of the world." He reached over and patted her knee without taking his eyes off the road.

CHAPTER 11

A SMALL DANCE

So far as good taste is concerned, the decorations for a ball cannot be too lavish or beautiful. To be sure, they should not be lavish if one's purse is limited; but if one's purse is really limited, one should not give a ball! A small dance...would be more suitable.
Emily Post, *Etiquette*

"I've been waiting such a long time for you," the frightened and happy girl seemed to say by her smile, shining through tears, as she raised her arm to Prince Andrei's shoulder.
Leo Tolstoy, *War and Peace*

Massachusetts can seem in a sullen sulk in July, and in those days before air-conditioning it was hard to sleep at night, twisted in damp sheets. And what was happening at Burnmouth? Burnmouth, sitting high on the lawn overlooking Frenchman's Bay, the salt breeze cooling its rooms and gardens. In the middle of August Zack and Katie drove back to Maine. In the trunk of the car were some posters from the Boston Museum, copies of real French posters. Nancy had instructed her to buy them for Katie's own coming-out party, scheduled for Labor Day weekend.

"Terrific!" exclaimed Nancy as they unrolled them. "Perfect!"

Each armed with a box of aluminum foil, mother and daughter spread out the ersatz Lautrecs, Degas's, and Steinlens on the floor of the Club's ballroom and scrunched silver foil frames around them. It was Nancy's idea to decorate Katie's coming-out party this way.

"They'll look terrific interspersed with big pots of red geraniums."

"You are so clever, Nancy," said Granny, "I never would have thought of that."

Everyone agreed it was typical of her mother to substitute wit and ingenuity for hiring professionals and spending a lot of money. And Katie noticed only fleetingly that money seemed to have become more and more of a concern. She was barely aware of all the new little economies because she was obsessed with a plan she had come up with.

She had invited Ian to her party. Toward the end of the hot Boston days it had occurred to her that, even though the invitations had already gone out, it might not be too late. After all, she told herself, it's customary for a family to summon both old and new friends to celebrate their daughter this one time before her wedding, and the wedding would obviously be too late. She herself wouldn't be inviting him, her parents and grandmother would be.

She thought of almost nothing else on the long ride north while Zack listened to the baseball game.

As soon as they had gotten to Maine she had called Tom for Ian's address, and she wrote it on the envelope herself. Or envelopes, plural, as the first two had to be torn up.

"I doubt he'll come." said Tom, "He's been travelling in France. I don't know if he'll be back."

For over a week Katie listened for the mailman's car coming down the driveway and after riffling through the bundle she would sink back into dull expectation for the rest of the day. One morning Nancy got to the door first and she had a slightly nervous smile on her face when she handed Kate the ecru envelope with the Canadian stamp. Kate tore it open, almost destroying what was inside.

She had to read it twice to make sure, but there was no mistake; it was clearly written on the ecru card in neat black handwriting.

"Ian Hart Douglas accepts with pleasure Mrs. McAllister's and Mr. and Mrs. Bowman's kind invitation for a small dance

73

in honor of Katherine Lewis Bowman...." And then the date, time, and place, all perfectly correct.

Katie looked up at her mother and Nancy could tell from her expression how much this meant to her.

"I'm so happy for you," she said and gave Kate's shoulder a fleeting hug.

Katie's longing to see Ian cut through all the other excitements of the days leading to September second. But because Winifred White was giving the dinner party at the Club before the dance and had limited the guest list to fifty close relatives and old friends, Katie hadn't dare ask if he could be invited. Thus she wouldn't start expecting him until after ten o'clock and could enjoy herself until then.

Katie "looked like a million dollars" in the white dress that she'd found in Boston. It was actually from Filene's basement, and Katie was proud that it had cost less than twenty-five dollars. (She hadn't wanted to ask Nancy for money.) It had a low scalloped neck, and a full skirt that made her waist look tiny. The matching shoes, also from Filene's, hurt a bit, because they were cheap. She wore a gardenia in her hair—at least in the beginning. But it kept falling out so she left it beside her dessert plate. Clearing the table, the divinity-school waiter picked it up and put it in his pocket.

All around her, guests in their best summer garb chattered their enthusiasms. Katie was happy, she loved the attention, but when for a second or two she let her smile drop those who knew her well might see that she was also worried. What if he didn't show up after all? All the excitement, all the buildup— and this perhaps her last chance to see him ever.

"What a lovely party, really the best all summer."

"And so many people from all over. Where on earth have they all come from?"

"Probably people Katie went to school with, and probably people Nancy and Zack went to school with, too."

"And of course cousins and aunts and uncles, what a wonderful mix of ages."

"Aren't the flowers divine!"

Most of the older ladies commented on the flowers. There were pinks and reds and corals: roses and lilies and huge hydrangea blossoms beginning to turn rosy.

At dinner the men made toasts.

"To our own little Katie McAllister." (The speaker seemed to have forgotten that Nancy had married Zack Bowman.) "Nearly as beautiful as her mother, who is nearly as beautiful as her mother!"

Twitters, giggles, and groans greeted this.

"And you know, ladies and gentlemen, I am referring to our own counterparts of Elizabeth Taylor, Helen of Troy, and Aphrodite herself!"

"Odd conception of mythology," a male voice whispered loudly.

Old cousin Sebastian, in a dove gray dinner jacket, marched a smiling Katie around the dining room on his arm, showing her off to the different tables while people clapped. She hoped Ian had come early and was outside the dining room's French doors.

The tables began to be cleared, and the ladies went to the ladies' room where they waited impatiently in front of the two (only two!) stalls, gossiping and exclaiming how lovely everything was though only God knew why there were only two stalls. Soon Katie, Nancy, Daddy, Granny, and the family boxers Brutus and Angelica—gardenias dangling from their collars—were lining up to greet the guests. ("So like Zack to have dogs in the receiving line!") They could hear Harry Marshard's band playing in the ballroom a medley of Cole Porter and Hammerstein songs, the fat drummer growling, "I get no kick from champagne, flying so high with some guy in the sky is my idea of nothing to do...."

Half an hour later Katie had shaken every possible right hand, and still no Ian. She was determined not to be disappointed but it was difficult. The band struck up "K-K-K-K-Katie" as they always did when she entered the room, and she let her father sweep her away in the first dance. Everyone else cleared the floor and watched them. They danced well together, the eighteen-year-old and her renegade father. They looked alike, graceful people with big eyes, dark curls, sensual mouths; almost gypsy looks. Enemies of a sort, lovers of a sort, mentor and student, parent and child, they were everything a father and daughter could possibly be to each other.

The band whipped up a froth of favorite songs including "The Most Beautiful Girl in the World," "Once in Love with Amy," and "My Heart Belongs to Daddy"; the musicians knew these were good dancers and they played faster and faster. Katie could see in the swirling mass that people were smiling at them with affection or perhaps even admiration. Then they played "When I'm Not Near the Girl I Love, I Love the Girl I'm Near," and she wondered how many smiled because it was Zachary Bowman, for whom those words were all too true, who was dancing with his daughter.

The faces were going so fast that Katie couldn't distinguish whether perhaps one of them was Ian's. Was she imagining him over by the main door? Finally, with a big drum roll, the band stopped so everyone could clap and cheer. Zack bowed to her and she curtsied as she had been taught to do for the cotillion. Looking up, blushing, smiling, overheated, she saw Ian. He came into focus, standing at the main door with a glass of champagne, watching her. Smiling at her. He looked wonderful in his white dinner jacket, even more sleek and handsome than she remembered.

She was about to wave, but Zack Bowman had seen him too, and grabbing Katie's hand perhaps a little roughly, he led Katie to the opposite end of the room to where Granny and Nancy began clapping again. He deposited her in front of Uncle Peter, who was lazily eavesdropping on a conversation between Margaret Louise van Linden and Mrs. Andover White, each in droopy lace and big white shoes. Dear Uncle Peter, he was already quite pink in the face, and ordinarily she would have loved to dance with him. He dutifully put out his cigarette and struggled to his feet, taking Katie in his arms. Now it was harder to see Ian as Peter pushed her around to an old-fashioned waltz, a lovely waltz that she so much hoped Ian would cut in on.

But Ian didn't cut in. He was still standing there watching as far as she could tell. Cousin Sebastian cut in and then some other older men danced with Katie after that. They probably wanted to get it over with before settling down to the serious business of getting drunk. The younger men apparently respected their elders' "droits de seigneur," and it seemed forever that she was whirled and stumbled and pushed around until finally Ian cut in.

CHAPTER 12

TATTOO ISLAND

[A]bout 400 million years ago, the three oldest rocks on Mount Desert Island—Ellsworth schist, Bar Harbor Formation, and Cranberry Island Series—had formed. At this point all three rocks were part of an ancient continent called Avalonia, lying somewhere between North America and Europe in the Iapetus Ocean. But slowly, as tectonic plates shifted, North America and Avalonia started moving toward each other, and eventually the two continents collided.
James Kaiser, *Acadia: The Complete Guide*

There was a familiar summer sound, a sort of swishing sound, that had puzzled and enchanted Katie since she could remember. It was slightly rhythmic, almost like breathing, and if she hadn't heard it often late at night she would have assumed Higgins the gardener was mowing the lawn back and forth below her window. But she knew it was either the wind in the leaves or the wavelets inhaling and exhaling upon the pebble beach, or sometimes a car taking the curves as it crunched down the gravel driveway. Now, the afternoon after her party, Katie sat very still in the front hall and waited to see what the noise would turn out to be. It got louder, and then stopped. She rushed to the window and pushed the organdy curtains aside to see Ian emerge from a convertible. She didn't wait for him to ring; she didn't want Agnes to come fuming in from the pantry.

"May I come and say hello and goodbye to you tomorrow?" Ian had asked as they danced the night before. She had hardly been able to sleep, the excitement of the party and the excitement of seeing Ian sandwiched into one short night. She had refused the daytime events planned for out-of-town guests by saying she felt sick. The others had gone off to brunches and luncheons, leaving her alone in the house. Except for the Household, of course.

He stood before her in blue jeans and a black turtleneck sweater, his dark hair tousled from the convertible. He took her hand, kissed it, and then kissed her on the forehead. They were such tender little kisses she wondered if they were the kisses of a brotherly friend or something more.

"The belle of the ball," he said, then he raised her chin in his hand and looked into her eyes as though he would find the answer to a whimsical riddle there. "Little Katie, all grown up. You were beautiful last night and you're even more beautiful now."

"Thank you," was all she could think to say. She hesitated. Flustered, she decided not to ask him in. Where would they sit? And Agnes would be rattling around in the back, wondering what they were up to. He seemed to sense her hesitation.

"Let's walk," he said reaching out his hand. "Show me Burnmouth. Show me your favorite places."

The air had a hint of autumn in it and the light a softness. Small clusters of red leaves contrasted against rusty greens, against dark evergreens, against the brilliant blue sky; taking his hand she felt she was stepping out into a new and not quite real world.

She called to Brutus and Angelica, who were always ready to join adventures, and they bounded along beside her wagging their stubby-tailed rear ends.

Katie, Ian, and the jumping dogs crossed the grass circle and climbed the steps into the woods. The path was narrow through the ferns and lily of the valley leaves. As her bare feet hopped from one flagstone to the next she thought of how he must be watching her from behind. Did he think she was fat? Should she slow down? No, she sped up, envisioning herself as one of those Walt Disney butterflies leading the prince along.

They crossed the weed-cracked cement floor where the garage had been burned by the Great Fire. She wanted to tell him about the fire, how it had happened the autumn she was twelve and had taken so much: grand estates, huge hotels, and whole mountainsides of trees; how luckily Burnmouth, the house and most of its woods, had been saved because the townspeople loved Granny and the coast guard kept spraying the roof. How the fire had, in a way, marked the end of her childhood.

"The big forest fire burned the garage in '47," was all she managed to say.

"I remember reading about the fire," he said.

"Mummy and Daddy came up and helped."

"Helped?"

"I mean they came up from Boston and Daddy took pictures and Mummy worked with the Red Cross."

"It must have been devastating."

"The garage burned and our wonderful old wooden station wagon burned too—you can see some parts over there. We kids loved it so, we all hung out the windows, when we were driven into town, all nine of us plus some dogs. It was probably dangerous but no one worried in those days."

"No, of course not," he said. Nothing more.

As she led him to the vegetable garden, their conversation refused to flow naturally. She pulled up a radish, spraying dry dirt on their feet. She handed it to him and he took a bite as though it were an hors d'oeuvre at an embassy cocktail party while his eyes held hers, an amused look on his face. Then he tossed it away.

"Sometimes I used to pull up whole cabbages and chomp into them!"

He laughed. "I'm sure it gave you lots of immunities."

Was she behaving like a complete idiot? She couldn't think of anything intelligent to say; somehow only ridiculous things were coming out of her mouth.

They plunged into the sweet-smelling meadow that led to Eden Street, the meadow where the old farmhouse had burned. She always wondered if she would meet a snake there.

"A mean old farmer had a house here once, and when we were little we were terrified of him but he died and we used to sneak in and steal ashtrays and jelly jars."

"Shame on you."

"Under the porch we found a nest of baby skunks. They were unbelievably adorable. We begged and begged but the grown-ups wouldn't let us get them de-stinked. De-stunk."

"I can imagine. I've always been partial to baby skunks myself."

Oh dear, she thought, was he being arch, making fun of her? What a ninny she was acting, like a toddler when more than anything she wanted to be worthy of this man. He had come all the way from Canada or maybe France on short notice to see her and here she was rattling on about baby skunks. He deserved someone glamorous and intelligent, and she could usually be so much better than this, yet something strange had happened to her.

They stood at the edge of the Eden Street sidewalk, on the gingerbread-like tar crumbs that lined it, and watched the cars speeding by, into town one way and toward the mainland the other.

"Do you want—" she blurted out. "Should I show you the place where I had my.... I know it sounds corny, but a secret place that I used to call the Enchanted Forest? There's a tree stump that I swear looks exactly like a miniature castle in a fairy tale."

He looked at his watch.

"I've never taken anyone there before." Nor had she ever told anyone how she crossed Eden Street and ducked under a rusty chain to trespass in someone else's woods.

"Show me whatever you like, but my plane leaves at five and I have to get the rental car turned in first. I don't know what the traffic will be like."

"The beach is more important," she said, turning and leading him down the Burnmouth driveway. The beach was more spectacular, easier to impress someone with, and she was a little relieved not to show him that most private place, which he might not understand. Back on the driveway they stood on the wooden bridge and looked down at the trickling stream, the water sparkling around miniature islands of stones on its way to the bay.

"Burnmouth is named after this stream, because the old-fashioned word for stream is b-o-u-r-n and down there, past the trees, is where its mouth is."

He hugged her shoulders and that relaxed her a bit.

"Bourn also means boundary, because streams were often boundaries," he said. "As in 'the undiscovered country from whose bourne no traveler returns.'"

She loved those words and they terrified her. Should she tell him that, should she tell him that she knew he was quoting Hamlet?

But she didn't want him to think she was showing off.

"Right," she said.

They left the driveway and went down another path under the tall cedars that separated Burnmouth from the estate to the south, and this brought them beside the servants' quarters. They didn't linger but crossed quickly to the far side of the lawn, the opposite side from the formal garden. Here and there early autumn leaves lay on the ground.

"You remember the garden party that day before we went to the movies?"

"I do. I remember you standing at the bar before you absconded to the beach."

"Oh," she said.

"You looked wonderfully out of place in your little black dress. Like you'd escaped from a French movie."

She laughed and dared to take his hand.

"Come and see our Pretend Town."

She led him to the biggest rock, an outcrop at the bottom of the great lawn. The rock was one of the few ways one could get to the beach and the only way to maneuver was on one's rear end. So she let go his hand and they slid their way down to the beach.

As always, the beach felt like a different world. Here the air was fresher, the sky was immense, the sea, deigning to lap at the edges of rocks and pebbles, was in full command. The wind seemed to have blown away all traces of houses, gardens, lawns, woods, and people. Seagulls swooped and dipped and called to each other. Farther north, up the beach, the only suggestions of civilization were boulders piled up for the foundation of the still-unfinished ferry dock.

All of it had been a theatre for the imaginations of the McAllister children. How wonderful now to have an audience to show it to.

"This rock was the hotel in our Pretend Town that my cousins and I invented when we were kids. I was the mayor."

"Not very comfortable beds in your hotel, I shouldn't think."

"Oh no, very comfortable! I could sleep forever on these rocks!" She didn't describe how she loved to taste their saltiness with her tongue, loosen her body so there were no sharp edges beneath her, close her eyes until there was only warmth and breeze and the sound of the ocean.

Each rock had its own personality, but she didn't try to explain that to him either. She pointed to rocks big enough to hold five or six children at a time.

"That one over there was the general store and that was the post office and that was City Hall."

"A great place for a childhood."

"I loved it here. More than anywhere."

He took her hand and they walked a little further before he stopped again.

"I did a little research before coming here," he said, sounding professorial. "Where we're standing is called the Bar Harbor Formation."

He kicked the side of the general store.

"Siltstone and sandstone, probably dating from the Late Silurian period."

"The Late Silurian period? When was that?"

"Over four hundred million years ago. Did you know that the first plants appeared on earth in the Silurian period? The first living things."

"How do you know that? How does anyone know that?"

He put his arm around her shoulders as though he were going to take her into a great confidence.

"Rocks are like books, they tell the planet's history. They're moving, too, and as they move they leave behind all sorts of clues. Even though they'll be here for a hell of a lot longer than we will, they won't be here forever either."

Neither said anything for a while and she thought how different their views of the beach were. He reached his hand up to her face and touched the side of her cheek.

Flustered, she pulled away slightly.

"So you like geology?"

"Geology is a hobby of mine."

"Are you going to be a geologist?"

"I would love to be a geologist and I'm taking courses. But there are other things I need to know."

"Like what?"

"Political science and business."

He took her hand, kissed its palm and let it go.

At that moment she knew that, in spite of her awkwardness, his affection for her was something else besides brotherly. She couldn't think for a minute.

"Oh. Political science and business?"

"I've decided to be a good son."

Shy and scared and happy, she picked up a stick and poked around in the pebbles. She wanted to ask him what he meant about being a good son but she felt constrained. Her questions might sound dumb, she might not understand the answers. She still couldn't really think so she pointed out a tide pool, a miniature landscape with tiny, shelled creatures and frilly plants. Their backlit reflections trembled in it.

"Were you a good mayor?"

"I was tough. I annoyed my sister and cousins."

"In political office one has to annoy occasionally."

"I owned the general store and sold the other children stuff I found. We used sea glass and bits of pottery for money. Blue and white designs. Always blue and white." She was talking much too fast. "Those long shiny seaweed things with tails and ruffled edges were worth a lot."

He was laughing. He seemed to approve of her childhood.

"And I gave tattoos."

"Will you give me a tattoo?"

"You'll have to pay."

"How much?'

"Something pretty that you find."

He investigated the high tide line of dried seaweed, broken shells, and bits of debris. Brutus and Angelica helped, sniffing things.

"How about this?" He handed her a little scallop shell.

"That's perfect." She put it in the pocket of her windbreaker. She would keep it forever. "But we have to do it on Tattoo Island."

She found some charcoal and a smooth stone. Then she took his hand again and they stepped over the agitated bit of ocean that was swirling around the rock called Tattoo Island.

"I'll do it on the back of your hand," she said.

"Put it on my cheek."

"What design do you want?" She could feel how hot her own cheeks had become.

"Let me think. How about a heart with an arrow through it?"

"Oh, come on," she laughed but she drew the heart on the stone. Though not the arrow. She pressed it against his cheek and he put his hand over hers and they both held the stone against his skin as though trying to stop a wound from bleeding. When he kissed her Brutus and Angelica barked and ran back and forth jumping and slipping. Her first thought was panic that someone might see them from the house. Then she let herself be flooded by happiness.

"Have you ever run into a silkie down here on your beach?" he asked. His other hand was at the back of her head playing with her curls.

"A what?" She was trembling. She was aching.

"A silkie. They're creatures that live in the sea and come onto land sometimes to fall in love with human beings."

"Oh, those things you sang about!" She remembered that night on the lawn three years ago, how he looked up at her before the last stanza. "No, not yet. At least not unless...."

And he kissed her again.

Later she suspected that someone *had* been watching; after all there were those binoculars on the veranda. Later still she wondered if that was why her father acted the way he did, if that afternoon he gained hard evidence that Ian was not going to be just another of Katie's summer crushes.

CHAPTER 13

MUD SEASON

Madame Merle tossed away the music with a smile. "What's YOUR idea of success?"
"...It's to see some dream of one's youth come true."
"Ah," Madame Merle exclaimed, "that I've never seen."
Henry James, *The Portrait of a Lady*

"No one can adequately express the exact measure of his needs... for human speech is like a cracked kettle on which we beat rhythms for bears to dance to, when we had hoped to move the stars to pity."
Gustave Flaubert, *Madame Bovary*

Katie was surprised to find that autumn in New York State could be as beautiful as in New England. The Vassar college campus and the land around it were as romantic as any lover could wish for. The trees turned magnificent colors and though the Hudson Valley didn't have an ocean, it had that enigmatic river, a river as evocative as any body of water she had ever seen. She knew that distinguished spirits haunted its mists, ghosts of explorers and nineteenth-century landscape painters; phantoms like Ichabod Crane and Rip van Winkle.

Ian drove up from Princeton many weekends when she didn't take the train down to him. They sought out secluded places, edges of woods, borders of empty fields, dead-end roads by the river. Cars had big front seats in those days, like sofas on wheels, with gearshifts politely holding themselves out of the way. A boy and girl could make themselves comfortable throughout most endeavors in spite of the difficult underwear. And their endeavors were tame by today's standards.

The respect that someone like Ian had for someone like Katie imparted to these endeavors a delicious aura of postponement.

It is hard to explain how sexy life was before the sexual revolution. Both guilt and daring were easier to come by in those days of boundaries. And flirtation and seduction made movies, novels, songs, musical comedies, and operas glow.

Before the '60s blasted so much apart, there were boundaries between classes, nationalities, and ages. Children were dressed like children, and adults of the McAllister sort wore blue jeans only on boats and picnics. Women wore dresses and lived in terror of their slips showing. Or, God forbid, a bra strap! There was more privacy, and particularly there was more division between the sexes. Members of each had different agendas in life, and penetration by a man of a woman was a penetration of a boundary in every sense.

The Pill was yet to be invented and virginity on one's wedding night still considered an ideal. Katie had friends who were exploring a new promiscuity, or at least talking about it, but "shotgun marriages" were a disgrace and single mothers existed only in books, slums, or reform schools. The quest for abortions sent terrified young women to a Latin American country or a super-secret expensive doctor who called it something else—or to a coat hanger.

Between covering her face and neck with tiny kisses Ian told Katie stories, though she couldn't tell if they were his own creations or legends from French Canada or, before that, Scotland. They involved mythical creatures from the sea, tree spirits, and gnomes who lived in caves. His stories both delighted and sometimes frightened her.

"Do you have silkies in the St. Lawrence?"

"Oh yes, particularly powerful ones."

When Ian was feeling serious, perhaps as they sat in the car at night, his arm snuggling her against his big arctic-type jacket, he told her about his hopes for French Canada, his political ambitions, and his passion for geology. She listened like a loving puppy dog trying to understand its master. She was in awe of him; her days, her thoughts, her dreams were full of him, and her studying that freshman year was half-hearted at best. There seemed to be nothing more important in her life than Ian.

He played the guitar and sang to her. Sometimes he sang and played for a whole circle of her friends. The girls put aside their bridge hands and sat on the common-room floor, soft white knees hinged between Bermuda shorts and knee socks. The songs were always either Scottish or French, two cultures Katie found impossibly romantic.

"Your Ian is one cute guy," a classmate would say to her, or "How lucky you are, does he have a brother?" The freshmen girls were all new to the campus of course, still looking over each other, and over each other's wardrobes and friends, and she felt she had arrived with the most wonderful luggage of all. She was so proud.

At Christmas, instead of going to stay with Granny McAllister and make her Chicago debut at the big cotillion there, Katie wanted to be with Ian.

"What do you mean you aren't going to Chicago! You can't just quit like that," fumed Zack over the telephone.

"Granny will be disappointed," said Nancy who was on the extension.

"I know, I'm sorry, but I'm so sick of parties. I've already done Boston and Philadelphia and that one in Wilmington and those two in New York. And we've been invited by his parents' friends to stay in Georgetown, and I don't know Washington at all. Please, I may never get another chance like—"

There was a click on the Massachusetts end of the line.

"Did Daddy just hang up?"

"He's very upset. You know how much this means to him."

"What if I just go to Chicago for Christmas and then meet Ian afterwards?"

"And miss the cotillion?"

"Yes, Mummy, please."

They couldn't after all tie her up and make her do what they wanted, so all the invitations were regretted and Katie missed the cotillion. Zack Bowman had looked forward to his daughter being paraded in front of another city's rich young bachelors and he hardly spoke to her while they were all in Granny's Chicago apartment. Granny McAllister was disappointed not to be able show off her pretty granddaughter to her Chicago friends but she only bit her lip a few times and soon cuddled her "girl" just as much as ever. Nancy was the only one who didn't seem upset. Perhaps she was just being "philosophical about it," as she often advised her daughters to be, or perhaps because she liked Ian a lot; in any case, she understood. Of course Katie was much too young to get married, but this nice young man was, as she liked to say, a "keeper."

So Katie and Ian went to visit some friends of his family in Washington D. C. It snowed and the flakes were beautiful against the pastel houses in Georgetown. Ian's family's friends were State Department people, gracious and intelligent. The host had been an ambassador to a country Katie had never heard of. She was given a pretty guest room with flowered furniture, a cashmere blanket neatly folded over the arm of the upholstered chair. At breakfast she was shy with her host and hostess, who were polite but not interested in her. They obviously adored Ian and Katie suspected they thought she was not quite good enough for him. Did he perhaps feel that, too? Now that they had moved out into the bigger, realer world away from Burnmouth and the campus and the Hudson River, doubts began to penetrate the fog of her happiness.

After Washington they went skiing in Vermont. Katie, unlike most people she knew, had never skied before. They rented her skis in a warm little hut at the bottom of the mountain that smelled of sweet melted wax. Ian was particular that she find good skis, and good boots that really fit. When she was stood up in the boots she felt she had turned into an enormous wooden puppet and couldn't move unless someone pulled her strings.

Ian of course had his own skis (Heads, considered the best) and boots and all the necessary equipment. The paraphernalia seemed almost a second skin to him. He had been skiing in the Laurentians since he was three.

He patiently taught her the "snowplow" before they took the lift. This apparently countered sliding downhill too fast and was a way of stopping, sort of like bringing a sailboat up into the wind. What an awkward position, she thought, with pigeon-toed legs spread and the butt sticking out when you tried to move. It looked cute on the several toddlers who were also learning nearby.

Only when she had more or less mastered the snowplow did they take the chair lift.

"All right, off we go," he said, adjusting his goggles. The breeze was making little whirlwinds of white just off the ground; there was a dust of snow in his black hair.

Luckily the lift had two seats side by side. She watched the empty ones jerking inexorably toward them down the mountain and she realized she was shaking. She was terrified about getting on the horrible thing, which didn't really stop for you; it was like becoming part of an assembly line. And with her whole lower part weighted by these strange encumbrances, what if she fell? She managed, though, and as soon as the chair hit the back of their legs and they were scooped up with a great swinging motion, her mitten grabbed Ian's knee.

"Relax," he said.

She tried to relax, looking down at the lovely chiaroscuro of snow and trees below. And then below was farther and farther away as they were swung up higher and higher. God, she hated heights! It was so silent, the only sound came from the towers, whose whistling would grow louder as they approached, then turn into noisier and noisier clacking, before they were dropped down into semi-silence again.

Yes, it was beautiful, beautiful in a way she had never experienced before, and yet terrifying.

For three days they went up the mountain. In the evenings they drank and ate with Ian's friends in the warm cozy lodge that smelled of wood smoke and ski wax. They drank hot cocoa after skiing and later delicious hot toddies with cinnamon and melted butter. Ian's friends were French Canadian and very nice to her, except when they spoke to each other in French. The women were good-looking and sure of themselves.

Ian continued to teach her to ski.

"Don't be afraid to keep your weight on your downhill ski. Be flexible, think of it as dancing."

It wasn't like dancing. The only music was the menacing sound of the wind. And there was no one holding you.

"Watch me, try to do it the way I do."

She watched. He stopped and turned to watch her. She tried. But the tips of her skis (they were so long!) crossed over and down she went.

He wasn't smiling when he reached his arm to help her up. But he was patient and they tried again and again.

On the fourth day he said, "Now you know the basics, you just have to practice."

"Go," she said, "I don't want to hold you up."

Of course she didn't want him to leave her shivering alone on the windy mountain and have to make her way down alone in slow curves on the "Toll Road," the slowest, flattest, longest trail. But neither did she want him to see how miserable she was, what a failure she felt. She didn't want to call any more attention to what seemed to be a growing list of her inadequacies.

So she stood in shaky snowplow posture at the top of the mountain and watched Ian slalom down with his friends, who skied nearly as well as he. Smaller and smaller, he became a graceful dot zigzagging against the white mountain as though he were a natural part of it.

Settling back into her class routine after Christmas vacation, Katie sensed an increasing restlessness on Ian's part in their talks and letters. She knew him well enough to suspect he needed to move on. But at spring vacation she invited him to visit her family in their Boston suburb, and when he accepted her hopes revived.

If it had been a year earlier Ian would have visited their big white house with porch and pillars and an ancient apple tree. Moving to the lovely colonial town not far from Boston five years ago had been great for Carrie and Katie because there were other children much like them in their own lovely old houses. During the months between summers they could play touch football or tag in the street and no one worried. When they moved from the city she had her own room and she'd been allowed to pick her own wallpaper, a bright pink with pussy willows. Decades later, in a new century, she could still remember the smell of the glue with which it was pasted up. It broke her heart when they had had to sell that house; she had been so happy the years they'd lived there. It had still been a time of hope.

But Zack Bowman's forays into advertising, public relations, photography, travel writing, and arranging beauty contests for charities had not produced enough income to pay the mortgage and taxes. And Nancy's trust fund only went so far.

Looking back, Katie realized that it wasn't only their squabbles about paying bills that her parents endured in those days. It must have been painful for both Nancy and Zack to watch Zack's natural optimism wear away bit by bit. In the beginning he'd had promising employment; he'd done publicity for the Boston Symphony, public relations for the Museum of Fine Arts. But nothing he attempted seemed to work out. Other men were defined by either moneymaking jobs or inherited fortunes so vast that others' opinions didn't matter. Good looks, joke telling, tennis playing, charm, and goofy schemes defined Zack.

Katie understood all this only later, when she too was searching for a way to realize her hopes of a sparkling life. People like Kate and her father held tight to their dreams, their originality, their need for fun and glamour, but reality kept intruding.

But that March of her freshman year Kate had only Ian on her mind. She worried about him, worried that he was losing interest in her, and she worried about what he would think of them living in an ugly rented house in an unattractive part of the lovely colonial town.

"Perfectly dreadful" was a phrase Nancy and Granny often used to describe a soup served at a luncheon, or perhaps someone's dress. Nancy was too good a sport to use such a phrase about a place her family had to live, if only temporarily. But there was no question that the Victorian monstrosity was perfectly dreadful. Lacy doilies were scattered over the heavy furniture like scabs, and not enough light to read by came through the bashfully fringed lampshades. Katie knew that these dark rooms revolted her mother, and the house cast a pall over them all. Katie felt her family was living underwater, muddy water. Zack's guilt caused him to stay away a lot to avoid Nancy's wounded gaze.

Carrie, who was going to the local high school, had a huge crooked-floor bedroom under the eaves and when Katie came home from college they had to share. Early spring in New England is "mud season," a horrible monochromatic time, and to Katie the prospect of Ian coming to visit was the only bright light in the world.

Nancy and Katie showed Ian to what had once been a maid's room off the kitchen. Nancy was gracious as always, asking how his trip was, was the traffic bad, how were his studies going, and so forth. Then she left Katie alone with him saying she had to get back to her stew. The smell of the onions and spices was very strong in Ian's room.

"I'm sorry," said Katie as he put his suitcase down and looked around at the faded wallpaper with brown damp spots and the tiny sink in the corner. "It's a big house, but it doesn't have many bedrooms."

Her father had been adamant that Ian not be allowed to sleep above the first floor.

"It's fine," said Ian and he kissed the tip of her nose. "Is there a loo?"

The maid's bathroom was being used to store the Bowman's good china and glass, and the powder room in the hall was quite far away.

"I'm so sorry," she said again. "But you can use the shower at the top of the stairs when you need to."

"Let's go for a drive, show me the town."

She showed him the tree-lined streets where shutters framed windows of symmetrical old houses, and shell designs in glass hemispheres crowned their front doors; but when they drove by the house in which the Bowmans had recently lived she didn't point it out. They drove around in silence, past the village green, the old churches, the fortress-like jail and the ancient graveyard. Finally Ian said, "Do you have a river?"

The area around the river was industrial and a lot of the bank had been concreted over for parking lots. They found a secluded area near a bridge where some derelict bushes were decorated with trash, and Ian parked there. He held her, kissed her, and made her forget the miserable house she had brought him to in this miserable month of March. Or almost forget. Something more than the house was wrong.

They ate dinner on the ornate dining room table with the bulbous legs. Nancy couldn't find a tablecloth she liked enough, so better the scratches, stains, and cigarette burns of the old table. The dishes and silver-plated spoons, forks, and knives weren't her taste either and tonight she mourned more than ever her Georgian silver and Spode dinner plates, all of which had been packed away by the moving company in shredded straw and sealed cartons. Now, as much trouble as it might have been to dig them out, she regretted that she hadn't. She felt bad not only for herself but for her daughter, who obviously wanted to impress this nice beau of hers.

Zack Bowman made things worse. Much worse. He hardly greeted Ian, and Ian held out his hand a few beats too long before Zack shook it. From then on Katie's father ignored him. Nancy, the woman who could steer a boat through any storm, used all the power of her upbringing to get them through dinner. She kept the conversation going and it became almost a tête-à-tête between her and Ian as she asked him about his family, his life in Canada, and the courses he was taking. Katie learned information about Ian that she had never extracted herself. His father's family had been in mining for years, and was originally from Scotland. His mother was French. He knew he would go into the family business someday but first he hoped to work for the Canadian diplomatic corps because he loved traveling, and the histories and politics of different countries fascinated him.

"Perhaps you will become an ambassador," said Nancy.

He smiled his wonderful smile. "I would like that."

"I'm sure you would make an excellent one."

At this Zack snorted rudely. Up until now he had contributed nothing to the conversation. Ian and Nancy ignored him.

"Thank you," said Ian. "I have law school to look forward to first. And this summer I was lucky to get an internship in Ottawa with a member of Parliament."

Ian was as charming as Nancy, and he asked her questions in turn. He had heard she was a wonderful sailor, understood celestial navigation and that sort of thing. Katie admired their poise and ease in a bad social situation. They're both pros, she thought. Katie made the sullen Carrie serve the food and clear the table with her, terrified that Nancy would do it and Ian be left alone with their father.

"What's for dessert?" asked Zack Bowman.

"I made a pie," said Nancy, smiling broadly, "an apple pie. I think it turned out quite well, actually." She started to get up.

"I don't want any."

Zack Bowman threw his napkin down and left the room. A few minutes later the front door slammed and they could hear his footsteps going down the porch steps.

"What is wrong with Daddy?" asked Carrie. It was the question Katie didn't dare ask. But she knew. Zack Bowman couldn't stand to have his oldest daughter in love. Not with anyone probably, but certainly not with Ian, enigmatic Ian from French Canada, who had caused his daughter to give up the Chicago coming-out parties. Ian, the wog.

"I'm afraid your father's had a bit of a reversal in one of his projects," said Nancy as she calmly carved up the pie and handed out platefuls to those left at the table. "Any one like a bit of vanilla ice cream with it?"

Ian offered to help Nancy with the dishes but she insisted she enjoyed doing them alone, and there weren't that many anyway. He and Katie should go off to the movies, or perhaps for a drive. (They had no television in the house—TV was only beginning to be a part of American life—so that was not an option.)

So they drove back to their place by the river.

Maybe it was to make up for the unpleasantness of the evening that their lovemaking went further than it had either in Poughkeepsie or Princeton. It had been so tame, really. Now maybe it was Ian's well-disguised anger that caused him to be a little rough. Almost as soon as he turned off the motor he undressed Katie from the waist up. She was surprised, usually he was so tender and patient. And he had never exposed her nakedness like this, usually he disturbed only parts of her clothing, undid buttons, raised her skirt on one side, slipped a blouse off one shoulder, reached his hand inside to caress a hidden breast. Once or twice he had spread her thighs and found her clitoris. He had guided her hand to his covered penis but had never undone his fly. Sometimes she even wondered if he had other girls for real sex and she was only a doll that he played with out of affection but not lust. If she hadn't been so scared perhaps she would have encouraged him more, but she told herself she liked the idea that he was saving her, and that she was saving him, for something later.

Now she was shivering in the car, her skin soft against the scratchy upholstery, white against the dark, exposed and open to the night and open to Ian, who had never seen her this way before. She sat up as straight as she could, breathing hard. He grabbed a handful of her hair and kissed her all over her face, her neck, her collarbone, her breasts. He lifted her rump with one hand and with the other pulled her skirt up, thrust his hand between her thighs and tugged to one side the crotch of her underpants. His finger was working its way into her when suddenly there was the sound of a car's motor and a bright light. The motor went dead but the light stayed on. It bathed the backs of their heads and their shoulders, and hers were naked. They heard a car door slam. Ian pushed her down into his lap, reached over her to turn the key, gunned the motor, swung the car to one side, backed up almost to the water's edge, completed the turn, and sped away.

He drove fast and crazily, down one street and then another, squealed around corners and out into the country. He kept looking up into the rear-view mirror but there were no lights behind them. By the side of the road near a pasture he helped her dress.

She was disheveled, very disheveled, her hair a mess, her lipstick smudged. She was shaking. When they got back to the house they sat in the car neither saying anything for a few minutes.

"You okay?"

"I guess so." She was trying to see herself in her compact's mirror.

They had gotten out of the car and were on their way to the porch when Zack Bowman drove up. He screeched to a halt and sprang out of his car, slamming the door. Then he took the steps two at a time and stood with his back against the front door, his arms folded like a sheriff in a cowboy movie. He didn't move and he didn't speak. Katie and Ian stood below him and then slowly climbed the steps.

"Let us in, Daddy."

He still didn't move. The door opened behind him and Nancy was there too.

"Zack, what on earth are you doing? Let them in."

Zack Bowman moved to the side and as Ian came up to the door Zack hissed, "Leave my house this minute and if I ever lay eyes on you again I'll kill you."

Behind him the dogs were growling.

"Allow me to get my things, sir," said Ian coolly.

Zack Bowman stomped off to the library and slammed the door.

Ian went to his room. In the hall Nancy hugged Katie for a long time. Katie was crying.

"Go with him," said Nancy. "Take him away from this dreadful place."

"I don't know if he wants me."

Katie lifted her wet face and over Nancy's shoulder saw that Ian was watching their embrace. She didn't know how long he had been standing in the doorway with his valise, his coat over his arm. She buried her face against her mother again.

"I want you," Ian finally said. She turned and tried to read his expression, but she couldn't.

"I'll stay in a hotel tonight and we'll go to Princeton tomorrow. I'll pick you up whenever you say."

Nancy released Katie and none of them said anything for a long minute. The dogs watched, panting slightly.

"If I were you," said Nancy finally, "I would go early. I'm sure Zack didn't mean a word he said, he's just a big spoiled baby, he'll get over it, but there's no point in letting him ruin your vacation."

Katie guessed Ian was as surprised as she by her mother's becoming an accomplice. But Nancy was serene and determined. She smiled at them both.

"Come back around 4:00, Ian; Zack is always sound asleep then. Katie, I'll wake you up in time."

Nancy woke Katie at 3:30 and made sandwiches for them while Katie drank coffee. In the sodden gray dawn Ian sat outside in his car waiting for her. They drove until the sun was up and then somewhere off the New Jersey turnpike they pulled over and fell asleep against each other. After they woke Ian continued driving but they didn't speak. When Katie dared to look up at Ian's profile it seemed stone-like, he seemed to be concentrating on the road and on something else, something internal. He frightened her and she kept quiet all the way to Princeton.

He got her a room at the Peacock Inn. He had a term paper to finish, he hadn't realized how much research he still had to do for it. He bought her a copy of *This Side of Paradise* by Scott Fitzgerald. She wandered around Princeton alone all day and in the evening, they went to a local pub. They ordered martinis with olives. There in the smoky orange light, at an initial-scarred wooden table with chewing gum stuck underneath it, Ian told Katie he didn't think that things were "going to work out" for them. Katie was stunned and yet not really surprised. She felt on the edge of begging, entreating, at least questioning, but she didn't say a word. She snuffled up her runny nose, stabbed at a tear with a cocktail napkin and sat very straight. You can't communicate with a phantom.

That house, that horrible house, it was as though it had put everyone in it under a wicked spell. Burnmouth had blessed her and Ian, and that horrible house had cursed them.

They spent their last night together in his bed in the Princeton dormitory—where if anyone had found her, he would have been expelled. They didn't, however, make love. His explorations of her body, his desire to claim it for himself, were obviously over. He held her and she cried. In the morning he returned her to the Peacock Inn.

CHAPTER 14

JIM

Blue Moon, You saw me standing alone
Without a dream in my heart,
Without a love of my own.
Rodgers & Hart, "Blue Moon"

"Well, if it isn't our very own Isabel Archer back from Rome!" Jimmy Morse, drink in hand, separated from the group around the piano and placed himself in front of her. "Wow, you look great, all that *sole mio* must have agreed with you."

"I hate Henry James," she said.

She did look different from the last time she'd seen him. When was it, exactly? Probably spring a year ago, her senior year, when he'd come to visit her at Vassar and ridden his bicycle straight down the hill into Sunset Lake. In Italy she'd let her hair grow longer, sometimes wore it up now, slightly sloppy on purpose. She hoped she resembled a brunette Brigitte Bardot. She wore lighter lipstick now, and darker eye shadow. Daddy had told her he didn't like her "new look."

They were at a Club dance but the band was taking a breather and some of the jollier young men were trying out their barbershop routines and making people laugh. "Swinging on the outhouse door! Without a shirt on!" And so forth. The general opinion was that they sounded like screech owls.

Katie Bowman and Jimmy Morse had known each other forever. When people asked them how they met they never knew how to answer. "Just socially, I guess." Perhaps it had been at one of the coming-out parties. Perhaps it was even before that, in Maine when Jimmy had been someone's houseguest. All the "privileged" East Coast children knew each other or knew each other's friends. They "summered" in or at least visited the same places: The North Shore of Boston, Cape Cod,

Newport, the Hamptons, and Mt. Desert Island. They had gone to the same boarding schools, the boys anyway, and the same colleges.

People liked Jimmy Morse and no one bothered to wonder about where he was actually from. He knew how to behave, and also how to misbehave, which was the main thing. He went to Yale, like most of the Chicago boys, not Harvard or Princeton, but that was good for Katie because New Haven was closer to Poughkeepsie and Vassar didn't admit boys in those days. And he was serious about his studies at Yale; he got good marks in spite of his devil-may-care attitude.

After Ian was gone it had been a bitter spring, and when Katie had come back the next fall it had almost been worse. She existed in a sad stupor for a long time. Vassar depressed her, particularly at the change of the seasons. The trees seemed heavy with sorrow, and there were parking spaces around the edges of campus so full of memories she took out-of-the-way paths to avoid them. Girls who had once admired her became indifferent. In classes she would sit in the back with her chair tipped against the wall and argue with the professor any time she dared. In order not to think when she wasn't studying she became a bit wild. She avoided signing up for classes that met on Mondays and Fridays and took the train down the Hudson to New York City a lot, and the bus to Vermont a lot to ski in the winters. Often she went alone. She met boys skiing and partied with them, and she drank more than she really wanted to. She couldn't help but keep an eye out for Ian while waiting in line for the chair lift. And she did become a better skier.

Jimmy Morse was one of the many boys who were happy to be wild with her. Riding his bike into Sunset Lake (beside which Vassar always held its graduations) was one of the tamer of his escapades. They had gotten drunk together more than once, driven too fast in that condition, skied in that condition, gone canoeing on a river still clogged with ice in that condition. More than once she had snuck off through the bushes at the edge of campus late at night (there were guards back then) to meet him. They had spent a lot of time in Poughkeepsie's workingmen's bars drinking dime beers.

They had spent a lot of time in New York City jazz clubs—including one where a British lady named Marian McPartland played the piano on a platform in the middle of a horseshoe-shaped bar. Jim knew a relic of an old speakeasy down some narrow crooked steps where, after four in the morning, when everywhere else was closed, you rapped on a door and got served drinks. There was a bar they liked just around the corner from Grand Central Station. When she had to go back to Poughkeepsie and he to New Haven, they would spend a couple of hours there before their trains left. On the walls were framed photographs of boxers (human ones) and it was nearly deserted on Sunday afternoons. It had all the womblike comfort of a good saloon, low light, a pleasant bartender, and in those days the television set was small, silent, and barely noticeable suspended in its corner.

Sometimes they talked there for so long they missed their trains.

They were both majoring in English and they talked about literature. He liked the authors she did: Joyce, Fitzgerald, Tolstoy, and particularly Conrad. He swore someday he'd read Finnegan's Wake, start to finish. They both liked what she called "juicy writing," sentences like music with lots of metaphor, plots that trembled on the edges of magic realism. Slightly sentimental literature. They liked Nabokov's *Speak Memory* and were excited by *Lolita* when it came out.

"All those arcane complicated words," said Jim.

"As though he put letters in a kaleidoscope and shook them up," she said.

"Nabokov's sentimental too—it's the way he disguises it that makes it so wonderful."

They talked about Hemingway, but she didn't admit that the main reason she liked his books was that she wished she were one of his characters, a Hemingway heroine, Lady Brett Ashley, Maria, or that nice nurse. Or even one of the heroes, one of the men. A bullfighter, maybe.

"Though that story about the bad guys in the diner," she said, "I don't see what's so wonderful about that."

"Jesus Christ, it changed American literature. No one ever wrote the same way again."

"I know, people always say that. The economy of language. I prefer mess."

It irked her a little that he knew he would be an English professor, and she had no idea what she would do.

The drinking age in New York State was eighteen, but Jimmy and Katie got good at lying in other states. Lying was something Katie always hated to do, and after she was twenty-one, she didn't do it much until later when she really had to.

She felt comfortable with Jimmy. He was almost like a brother, or at least a cousin. If she had to barf into her evening bag after drinking too much she knew Jimmy wouldn't mind. (What else were evening bags good for? They were so tiny.)

Jimmy wasn't bad looking either. He was tall, had curly reddish hair, blue eyes, freckles, and was athletic enough to sometimes beat Zack Bowman at tennis.

Jim's own father, it turned out, was a retired headmaster of a suburban day school in Hartford, and there was a certain amount of culture in the family. Much more culture than money. In fact the ratio was the reverse of most of the families she knew.

Now, fresh from her year of studying art in Rome, she had to admit to herself that she was glad to see Jimmy.

"You seem glum," said Jimmy and swung her out onto the dance floor when the band returned. "Gorgeous, but glum. I bet you've forgotten how to Charleston!"

The sons and daughters of the Summer Colony loved to emulate the Scott Fitzgerald culture of their parents. They listened to the same songs, danced the same dances. Many of them had never heard of Elvis Presley. Our American Dream, she thought, to be like Tom and Daisy Buchanan. But she was happy to dance again.

Katie had returned from her year in Europe in a funk. The culture shock was almost too much. She hated American supermarkets with their rows of over-packaged junk lit by fluorescent glare, she hated their inane music. She mourned the Italian greengrocers, butchers, apothecaries, and florists who wrapped one's daily purchase in soft gray paper. She hated driving again on boring highways in huge ugly cars. She hated towns scarred with parking lots and boxy architecture; she missed cobblestone streets and centuries-old buildings. She abhorred concrete, linoleum, plastic, Styrofoam, chewing gum. She complained endlessly, infuriating her father and boring everyone else.

"So you don't like Isabel Archer," Jim said a few days later, as they walked on Granny's beach accompanied by the boxers. He was skipping stones and the dogs thought he was doing it for them. They jumped each time he raised his arm and then followed the arc to the edge of the water.

Katie, head down, was searching for flat stones for him to throw. Under her feet there was such a variety of textures, colors, shapes, weights. The Bar Harbor Formation. Probably dating from the Late Silurian period.

"No," she said. "James is such a Bostonian. Everyone in his books is so uptight."

"So, if you wouldn't want to be an uptight Jamesian heroine, what heroine would you like to be?"

"Anna Karenina," she said. "I like her clothes."

"What about Emma Bovary? Do you like her clothes?"

"No. I don't like her or her clothes. Or her hair. Or her stupid husband. I think I'd like best to be Cleopatra. 'The sacred cat of Egypt,' according to Shaw. And you? Who would you like to be?"

"Leopold Bloom."

"Oh, come on. You're much too cute to be Leopold Bloom."

"I know I am. But I like the way his mind works. I like the way he likes eating kidneys. I like the way he's nice to his wife and the way he thinks about sex all the time."

"Do you think about sex all the time?"

"Only when I'm with you, baby."

"Sure."

Eventually Jimmy took her mind off her gloom. She knew in fact that he loved her, and she loved him too, after a fashion. He was fun. He was kind. They talked about everything, yet their silences were comfortable too. They did what the "Child Study" people (Child Study had been big at Vassar; her roommate had majored in it) called "parallel play." And though she was ashamed that this should be a part of it, she knew that even though he wasn't rich, her father liked him.

She wondered if she should she marry Jimmy Morse.

Before she endeavored to answer that question, Katie did one more impetuous thing, something more natural to a fifteen-year-old than someone seven years older. She'd had a lot of wine at dinner one night at Granny's and it made her nostalgic, for Italy, for Ian, for her childhood. She decided to walk on the beach in bare feet. It was a warm July night, warm for Maine anyway, a full moon almost obliterating the stars that scattered the sky. The second full moon that month, so a blue moon. She slid down the big rock that used to be the Pretend Town hotel, bunching her skirt to the side with one hand. It was her favorite skirt, too gypsy-like, too full and romantic to wear in public but fine for home. Or nocturnal walks. It suited her mood and she didn't care if it got wet or ripped.

The water was lapping the pebbles, repetitively, soothingly, seductively. Farther up the beach the lights from the ferry dock violated the night. The ferry was at its dock now waiting to leave again in the morning for Nova Scotia.

She crossed the beaches of the two estates north of Burnmouth, whose houses the 1947 fire had left in picturesque ruins. The town had lost so much of its tax base then, all those rich people abandoning their properties, it was inevitable that a ferry to Canada would be built; she'd heard that the planning began as early as 1949. And now, seven years after she and Michael Blake had first explored where the pier's foundations would be, the *Bluenose* was fully operative.

And what a great ship it looked, silhouetted against the evening sky! With its high black hull and huge red smokestack it could have been a smaller cousin to the ocean liners that had recently taken her to and from Italy. She imagined its decks and ballrooms graced by chicly dressed people drinking champagne, whispering in French and other foreign languages. She could almost hear the band playing.

Looming in the moonlight, it called her on.

In the pilings and the great cut boulders of the wharf's foundation she found niches she could pull herself up on and soon she swung her legs over the railing to gain the dock. No one had seen her—so far anyway, though the windows of the huge boat streamed light everywhere.

She tiptoed as though she were wearing high heels all the way to the gangplank that landed her on the deck of the ship itself. There was no one anywhere. The passengers must have disembarked earlier and whatever band she thought she heard had stopped playing. There was only the low rumble of some motor. She tiptoed around the deck until she came to an open door. She went in.

It was a large room, blaringly lit from overhead, almost institutional, and devoid of anything besides a large counter and some plastic chairs. She was about to proceed toward another door across from the one she entered when someone said, "May I help you?" It was a polite voice with a Canadian accent.

She smiled at the uniformed man.

"Oh, thank you, no," she said, "Just looking around." As though she were buying shoes at Saks.

"Well I'm terribly sorry," he said, "but we will have to ask you to leave. Regulations forbid anyone coming on board without first having passed through customs, passport control, and all that sort of thing."

"Oh." She wondered if she would be arrested.

"So I will have to show you out." He pronounced it "oot."

"Okay, I'm sorry. It's such a lovely boat though, I thought I'd have a look...."

His hand was gently under her elbow as he walked her out the door, around the deck, down the gangplank, and onto the pier.

"Thank you!" she called back to him as she ran to the end. Then she swung herself over the railing and scampered down to the beach. Looking back she saw his stiff figure against the night, obviously watching her.

She was soon clear of the boat's lights as she stumbled her way to Tattoo Island, the rock where Ian had first kissed her. Tiny diamonds of phosphorescence trimmed the edges of the water as it caressed the beach and rocks. She sat on Tattoo Island for a long time, her mind floating freely, not forming real thoughts, until she realized she was shivering with cold. Quite sober by then, she gathered up the wet hem of her skirt and made her way up to the house and to bed. She wasn't quite ready to admit it even to herself, but she knew she had made her decision about Jimmy Morse.

The next day people in town were talking about how some girl had tried to stow away on board the *Bluenose*. Higgins, Granny's gardener, knew all about it. He explained to people it was the Hillsburys' granddaughter, but he knew, and Katie knew he knew, that it was Katie.

CHAPTER 15

IN CARRIE'S ROOM

Pack up your troubles in your old kit bag
And smile, smile, smile.
George and Felix Powell, "Pack up Your Troubles in Your Old Kit Bag"

A fragrant breeze ruffled the organdy curtains and a late afternoon sun laid wobbly rectangles on the hemp rug. Katie, rocking slowly in the wicker chair with her baby son at her breast, wondered if this, Carrie's childhood bedroom, was better than hers. Katie's room had been her mother's once and looked out on the bay, the islands, the beach, garden, lawn, and oak tree, but Carrie's room had the western sun.

The baby's sucking, the lovely ache of her breast, was the most delicious sensation Katie knew. It was sexual, but in a solipsistic way, without the need for doing anything but hold a sweet-smelling soft bundle in one's arms. Nature, so clever with its seductions, had surpassed itself inventing this one.

Yet Katie felt she should be reveling more in being a mother, enjoying her little son more. Of course she did enjoy him most of the time. She loved the toothless smile that came so slowly as though he first needed to consider if he had good reason for giving it. She loved his chubby body with its graceful miniature limbs. And the tiny, tiny finger- and toenails, how could anything be so tiny?! Like a little chipmunk, she thought, the tiniest of the adorable summer mammals. Of course all of this was miraculously wonderful. But still. She ascribed her mood to being exhausted—not just by being awoken in the middle of the night, but by her new life among academics in Cambridge. She had had to suspend her art classes at the Boston Museum School and now would probably never have a career of her own. She would sit with the other wives and listen to the men talk.

The baby waved one tiny arm around as though conducting an invisible infant orchestra. He kicked his chubby legs at the painted light green table where out of his reach sparkled Granny's diamond bracelet. She had taken it off so the hard platinum wouldn't bite into his tender flesh and she hoped she wouldn't forget to put it back on.

Katie watched Hermione, her grandmother's old seamstress, smooth sheets of tissue paper on the bed as gently as if the paper too were a child.

Earlier Carrie's wedding dress had been folded inside the tissue paper. The dress had been Katie's a year ago and before that Nancy's and before that Granny McAllister had worn it with the veil of antique lace. Now the dress was on its way to a special dry cleaner in Boston, and then on to a cousin or perhaps a new generation. Carrie had dropped it on the floor an hour before, stepping out of it and into a pretty suit of robin's egg blue shantung. Then she and her tall (and rich) new husband had sped off in a balloon-covered MG.

Katie remembered when Hermione kept the family's clothes mended, brushed, ironed, and lovely, but now the elderly Swiss woman was called in only for special occasions. The Household had diminished long ago, doomed not by death alone, but by the economy—taxes mostly. Over the years a maid or two had been "let go." There was still a cook, but the laundress was dispensed with except for once a week, and the least conspicuous gardens surrendered to weeds for lack of a full-time gardener.

Katie pierced the silence in which both women had been wrapped.

"How long have you worked for Granny, Hermione?" She pronounced it "her meen" as they all did.

"Oh, my goodness, let me think." She had a German accent. "Since your mother was a baby. No, Miss Prudence had just been born. Ya, I remember Miss Prudence as a bitty bitty thing all wrapped up like a sausage. Master Peter not yet."

"Did they find you in Switzerland?" Katie immediately regretted the "find." People were always saying, "Where did you find your cook or your cleaning lady," as though these people were appliances. But Hermione didn't seem to mind.

"Ya, in Montreux. When the family was there for the waters. Mr. Peter senior, he was always looking for a cure, poor man. His legs."

Her grandfather's mysterious legs. Paralyzed from the waist down since his early thirties, they never did find out what was wrong with him. Even in the autopsy. She recalled the picture of him when he was younger, sitting in a delicate rattan wheelchair, smiling and holding high a glass of champagne.

"But now, only for grand occasions I come. I'm happy to see the family again. Good people your grandmother, and your mother too."

"We love to see you, too, Hermione—I wish you could be here all the time."

As the twentieth century lurched on, the accomplishments that had once been the province of professionals like Hermione had fallen to amateurs like Katie. Women of the McAllister's class, unless they somehow had retained their family money (and Old Money dried up as naturally as Old People did) or married into new money, found things slipping.

And now, much to Zack's horror, Jim had become a literature graduate student at Harvard. Zack had hoped Jim would detour into the business world, but he was clearly on his way to being a professor and so they'd never have a lot of money. Katie didn't think she'd mind, but still, it's hard to give up the all lovely little details associated with having money, she admitted to herself as she rocked in the sun-filled afternoon.

Hermione, Agnes, the other servants, her grandmother, her mother, her aunts, and their friends, Mrs. Andover White for instance, all those ladies of the former world were so accepting of their fates no matter how different from each other. And yet Katie couldn't imagine being accepting, she always wanted more, always more. Perhaps that was why she loved the idea of the blue moon.

As the child suckled she remembered her winter in Rome. Somehow the family had come up with the money for it, probably from Granny. She'd studied art there after college, and it was there that she'd begun to love drawing. Before that art had never interested her much, she had found her pictures through words; in her own head she illustrated the books she read. But the power of Renaissance painting and particularly the tenderness of Renaissance drawings showed her a new way of looking at the world. And when she learned how to make pencil or charcoal do her bidding, she saw that it was a way to capture things, places, and people, and to make them her own.

She had wandered around Spain, France, England, and Italy that first summer, or wandered as much as a well-brought-up woman was allowed to in those days. She had escaped the chaperones enlisted by her parents, she had followed whims, traveled with various young men she met along the way, all without losing her virginity. She smiled remembering how stubbornly she had refused to relinquish that bit of her deepest, most private self.

It wasn't fear that kept Katie, usually so adventurous, from succumbing to that particular destiny. Katie was a romantic and the one man who she was saving herself for had been nowhere in sight.

But even she could wait only so long.

When summer turned to autumn she had returned to Rome. As she sat drinking cappuccino her second day at the Accademia di Belli Arte a film student with tousled black hair asked to join her. He was wearing a black turtleneck sweater, had brown eyes and perfect features and though he was taller, there was no question that he resembled Ian. She didn't yet know anyone, and his lack of English didn't prevent him from becoming a sort of protector. She was grateful to him for teaching her Italian, and for showing her Rome, clinging to him as they wove in and out of the chaotic traffic on his Vespa. He was proud to show off not just the great piazzas, churches, the forum and coliseum, but the ruins that surprised at the sides of streets, in overgrown lots, in all sorts of unexpected places. He was teaching her so much and she delighted in learning it. While it was still warm they would speed down the Appian Way to the beach at Ostia, she hanging on for dear life, her hair blowing, her arms tight around his waist. Sometimes she laid her cheek against his back while the ancient trees sped by. And then winter came and one chilly evening in his tiny apartment, with its view of chimney pots and a sliver of the Castel Sant' Angelo, they made love.

That was another reason she had returned to America in a funk. It wasn't that she had had to say goodbye to her Italian lover and would never see him again. She had known from the beginning that she didn't love him enough to live a foreign life. But she had been young and free and he had made her feel beautiful; in those days so much had seemed possible. Maybe even Ian. Now, two years later, everything had changed; she had committed herself to marriage and being a mother, and she had to admit she was depressed.

These moments watching Hermione's rhythmic smoothing of tissue paper in the beloved old house were just what she needed. She drifted back momentarily to those soft summers when grown-ups arranged the Real World and all a child needed to do was daydream in the afternoon sun.

CHAPTER 16

TECTONIC DRIFTS

The world is nothing but a perennial see-saw. All things move without cease: the earth, the rocks of the Caucasus, the pyramids of Egypt, all sway with a common motion and their own. Constancy itself is yet another thing that moves, but it moves more slowly."
Michel de Montaigne, "On Repenting"

When Jamie was four and his sister, Nessa, two, Jim came back to their Cambridge apartment one late afternoon with what he thought was good news.

"I have a job offer. A half-decent job offer from a half-decent college. More than half, seventy-five-percent decent, actually."

"That's great. Where?"

He told her about the liberal arts college in New Hampshire, small but well respected, where he would not only teach English but also coach the La Crosse team.

Well, thought Kate, at least that will save me from a country club, suburban existence. It would be a rebellion of sorts. Living among people who live Lives of the Mind. She thought about the other boys she might have married and the lives she might have had with them. Michael Blake, for example, and his family's baronial estate in Pennsylvania. Or others who might have deposited her on Park Avenue like Carrie. Or Ian. No, she wouldn't let herself think about Ian.

And it would be beautiful. New Hampshire is almost as beautiful as Maine, she thought. She could not live in a place that wasn't beautiful.

So one day when the air was heavy with spring and the trees had become clouds of pink, white, and pale green, Kate, Jim, their children, their dog, and all their belongings moved to a small New Hampshire town.

The tarnished numbers over the front door announced that Twenty-Five Washington Street had been built in 1860. It was a wooden house painted a now-flaking white, and its gray shutters looked tired of holding themselves flush with the window frames. The front door was a faded blue, scratched, and sad. Kate's first thought was that she would paint the door red someday.

Except for some gnarled old apple trees on one side there had been nothing much in the way of vegetation to greet them except a few scraggly forsythia bushes along the front path.

The other houses on the street, all of the same period, could have been cousins or siblings to theirs, and were probably full of nice neighbors, Kate told herself. On balance it was all charming, she told herself. And it was real New England, not summer-colony New England like Burnmouth.

While the children and the dog bumped around investigating their new home, Kate collapsed on the sofa, which had been angled strangely by the movers in the middle of the living room, amidst boxes and crates and lost chairs. Exhausted, she closed her eyes and envisioned the world she would create. It would never be a Burnmouth, this crooked little house on less than an acre, but still. Imaginary hydrangeas, boxwood, cedar, and ivy settled across her view like an architect's transparency. She hoped she would have the energy to get started soon.

But first there was so much to do: finding the outlets for lamps so there might be light as dusk settled, even finding the lamps. Managing supper for her tired family. Jim, cheerful as usual, took Jamie with him to find a pizza place, or hamburgers, anything. It being a college town they came back with pita and hummus, olives, sprouts, and juice.

While they were gone Kate poked around with sleepy Nessa in her arms. The wooden floors seemed tired too. They tilted this way and that ("all old houses settle," the real estate lady had chirped), and gave the refrigerator door trouble closing because it had to go uphill. The kitchen had much too much linoleum, but never mind. The wobbly windowpanes made the view outside look like landscapes painted by a shaky hand. Dense woods at the back of the yard, which had seemed protective when they first saw the house, now seemed menacing. Would the dog disappear into them? The children?

Eventually Kate did paint the door red. She went to the hardware store (she had always loved hardware stores; they felt so optimistic, promising a fix to anything and everything) and brought home little rectangles of red paper. She laid them out on the kitchen counter and after a few days decided on a color called "Happy Tomato," though Jim had liked "Desert Sunset" and Jamie (naturally) "Fire Engine Red." A sunny enough day finally came and she painted once in the morning and again in the afternoon. Of course the new Irish setter puppy sniffed it when it was still wet and she had to pick the acrylic splotches off his snout. The door looked cheerful, the tiny boxwoods she had planted looked healthy, and she began to feel she was getting somewhere.

When she got discouraged again she would call Nancy and complain.

"It will never end! Just as soon as I get one thing fixed I have to tackle another. For instance, the toilet in our bathroom has come apart. The seat goes flying off to one side every time you sit down."

Nancy would come up to sleep in the cell-like guest room and take her shopping. There wasn't much to buy in the college town so they drove around the countryside for hours looking for antique stores. This gave mother and daughter time to talk, and as with her father years ago, Kate had imagined this might be an opportunity for her to get to know Nancy better. But Nancy was even less forthcoming than Zack; she was a listener, not a talker. And, in fact, they were both content with their relationship based on working together on practical projects, and putting a house in order was the perfect one. In the antique stores they never found exactly what they were looking for, but they found other treasures, and soon the house was full of spindly old chairs. They had fun rummaging through the swatches of fabric Nancy brought from Boston, ordering yardage and finding a local lady to stitch up pillows, curtains, and bedspreads.

The second year Nancy had Kate and the kids come and stay with her for three days in Boston while Jim was left to supervise the people who tore up the kitchen linoleum. Liberating the nice wood floor underneath was a present from Nancy.

Perhaps someday it would all mean something to her children, thought Kate, or maybe even her grandchildren, as Burnmouth had once meant so much to her. She was coming to love Twenty-Five Washington Street. It reminded her of a jigsaw-puzzle cottage, the perfect setting for her perfect children.

Kate adored their children, little Jamie and Nessa—actually "Vanessa," like Nancy; their nicknames had been extracted from the name of the same ancestress. They were beautiful children, funny and bright, and sometimes she couldn't believe that she and Jim could have produced such good-looking progeny. Jamie had limitless energy, seemed afraid of nothing, and made friends with everyone. He was always covered with scratches and bruises from his escapades.

"He's a real boy, Mrs. Morse," said the neighbors. As a toddler he went around pronouncing, "I'm a hacky little boy," and in second grade he announced, "I'm not going to let homework ruin my childhood."

Nessa, sensitive and feminine, took her lessons seriously and was his perfect foil. The times the three of them sat on the floor and colored, pasted, and cut paper with blunt scissors were among the happiest in Kate's life. Jim would come home to a kitchen covered with squiggles, rectangles, spirals, and confetti of red, blue, yellow, green, and orange, and dinner nowhere near ready.

"You are the Loch Nessa Monster!" shouted Jamie at Nessa, "and I am going to pull you out of the water so you will perish of affixiation!" and he chased his screaming little sister around the living room while the dogs followed, barking, their big Irish Setter tails knocking magazines, books, and the ashtray off the coffee table.

It was a healthy life with skiing and hiking up and down the hills and out into the farms. Her garden grew as she dug and planted, pruned and weeded, the dogs impeding her every move. In the fall the trees were beautiful, each one its own variation of red, yellow, orange, and gold lace, and in the winter the lake froze and they skated over ice embedded with twigs, leaves, and lost mittens.

Kate worked hard at being happy. This was her life, her grown-up life that she had looked forward to, and she wasn't going to waste it.

Her emotions reminded her of swimming in the ocean or a lake, currents of warmth and then of chill. She could never have said she was totally unhappy nor the opposite. And as when swimming, there was always the possibility of bumping into something. An electric eel for instance! And she would laugh at herself.

Yet often, in those guilty minutes when she knew she should bound out of bed and start the coffee, she would be almost paralyzed by emptiness. Once Jim had dropped the children off at school and gone to teach, she would be alone for the day, and what on earth was there important enough to do? Besides housework. She couldn't really get a job yet, not when the children would be home from school in a few hours and needed to be driven places, and fed, and all the rest. She tried setting up still-lives and painting them in the little room next to the kitchen but the apples and onions rotted and the whole enterprise bored her to tears.

"Pull yourself together," Nancy McAllister Bowman used to tell her daughters during their adolescent crises. "Stop feeling sorry for yourself," she'd say, and, worst of all, "Try to rise above it." Oh,

God, Katie used to think, that's so mean, so cruel! How could her mother not understand, why couldn't she soften a bit and sympathize instead? Didn't Nancy remember how important certain things were when one was a teenager?

But by the time Katie had become Kate and also Mrs. James Morse, wife of Professor Morse, her mother's annoying words began to make sense, and not only for teenagers. Nancy, she knew well by now, was not a mean or cruel person; she was a disciplined and courageous person and she wanted to fortify her daughters with what was actually very good advice. She was tossing them phrases with which they could pull themselves out of the swamps of self-pity.

Katie kept trying.

She thought she might write mystery stories like Margaret Louise van Linden. But in the peripheral vision around the typewriter things diverted her attention: a spider crawled across the desk; she must coax it onto a Kleenex and out of the way. What were the dogs barking at? She'd better go see. And maybe she should turn on the radio and get a weather report.

Jim came home one day and found her at the ancient Olivetti, scrunched papers all over the floor. He kissed the top of her head. "What on earth are you up to now?"

"Writing the Great American Mystery Story, what else!"

"My little dabbler, my little Hedda Dabbler."

It wasn't that Kate didn't have friends she enjoyed spending time with. Julie Covington, whom she had known in Maine, was originally from Chicago, like Granny. What a coincidence that they should both end up in northern New Hampshire. But Julie was not someone you could complain to. Her husband, Todd, now dean of admissions, was rumored to be the next president of the college, and as an administrator's wife Julie had social duties to perform. And because it was a time of strife on college campuses, Todd was always having meetings at their house. And they had four children to keep her busy, and they traveled.

Kate would have loved to join the students in their protest marches against the Viet Nam war, against racism, in solidarity with the public school teachers' strike, against the proposed shopping mall out on the highway, but as a popular professor's wife she felt she shouldn't. Besides she was not sure she had the energy.

"Try it," said Julie. "The worst that could happen is that you'll be arrested and Jim will have to go down and bail you out."

"And it will be written about in the Maple Leaf. I can see it: 'Police Drag English Professor's Wife by Hair as She Shouts Obscenities.'"

"I would join them if I weren't married to Todd. It would be fun— but not worth wrecking his career for. Your case is different, though. Jim is so admired as a sort of free spirit anyway. I'm surprised he isn't on the picket line."

"I don't have the right clothes."

"You are so completely silly! That's what I love about you."

"Maybe I'll go shopping for one of those long hippie skirts and some work boots."

"And beads. You need lots of beads and dangly earrings."

"I'll get a tattoo."

"Come on, Kate, cheer up. Give a party or something."

Another friend was Heather Anderson, an artist who worked in a studio on top of the Middle Eastern vegetarian restaurant. It always smelled delicious there, odors of cumin and garlic mingling with those of turpentine and strange glues. Kate loved to go see what absurd project Heather was engaged in at the moment. Heather affixed all sorts of gunk to her canvas— dried wheat and rice and gobs of something (it reminded Kate of the stuff Nancy used for depilating her legs) that hardened into brown Pollock-like swiggles. Kate liked Heather's work and she liked sitting on the paint-spattered floor talking to her, even though Heather didn't worry about the same things Kate did.

Kate had friends at the book club, too. They often argued about what to read next and eventually split off into two clubs, one taking up Proust and the other *Winesburg, Ohio.* Kate went with the Proustians, even though she thought Proust was a terrible bore at times, because the few men in the group had (surprisingly) insisted on Proust. There was no question about it; Kate had always been more comfortable with men than with women.

At home alone Kate read in Paul Goodman's *Growing up Absurd* that a woman found fulfillment in her children and didn't need "meaningful work." She wondered what this man meant by fulfillment. Whatever it was she didn't have it. Simone de Beauvoir and Betty Friedan comforted her that she wasn't the only unfulfilled woman in the world and she began to long for meaningful work to fill her emptiness. But she hadn't really been trained for any profession, unless one counted her aborted art classes. She had been trained to be charming, to dance well, to be a good dinner partner (which is why her father said she should read a lot), and a good hostess. Just like her mother, her grandmother, and Mrs. Andover White.

Some of the girls she had grown up with had taken up photography, child psychology, or real estate. Michael Blake had married a landscape architect and Jo, whom people had called a "Golden Girl," had a wonderful job doing something at Vogue. Carrie was involved with an art gallery in New York. In the larger world there began to be women reporters at newspapers, magazines, and on television. Television women dressed almost like men but in nicer colors as they read the evening news. Law schools began to accept more women students and some would even become judges—and not just in juvenile court.

Maybe if Kate had known more about geology she wouldn't have felt so guilty about those years of indecision. She might instead have enjoyed thinking of herself as a very sensitive seismograph, because between 1960 and 1968 most geologists came to accept the theory of plate tectonics. At the same time, the peace movement, the civil rights movement, the women's movement, and eventually the gay rights movement were knocking private worlds off balance. Strong tremors shook people and it was hard to adjust to the fact that their world had always been off balance and always would be. If Kate had known about tectonics, she would have loved the metaphor of their drifts, movement everywhere, in people's heads as well as below their feet.

One day Kate was sitting on Heather's studio floor with its hardened gunk splatters talking about all this while Heather stirred some strange potion over a can of Sterno. The smells of the potion and the cooking from the restaurant mixed in a way that made Kate wonder if she felt hungry or nauseated or both.

"Kate, you keep talking about all this unfulfillment crap but you never *do* anything about it. Are you really that depressed?"

"I don't know."

"Come on. You have two gorgeous children and a really nice husband. In fact he's one of the nicest people I know. And he adores you. How can that not make you happy?"

"I am happy—I mean, metaphysically. Just not quotidianly."

"God! Big words."

"I don't have talent like you, or your drive. I've always been such a dilettante."

"But you can draw. You draw beautifully. Get back to it. Draw real people at a life class somewhere. It might turn your life around."

Kate started attending a life-drawing class on Thursday nights. Two or three horny old men who couldn't draw also attended; the sight of nude females probably cheered them. She understood this because she had learned in Italy that drawing at its best was almost a sexual act; the instrument, whether pencil (the word came from the same root as *penis*), pen, charcoal, or #1 brush, caressed what the eye explored. Without fear. It was so private, so intimate. More than once when she drew, she felt on the verge of having an orgasm.

At home she drew her kids as they watched *Sesame Street*, she drew Jim as he slept in his big chair after dinner; she drew the dogs as they sprawled in the sunlight. Gradually, drawing began to erase her depression.

And then something extraordinary happened. A perfect stranger wanted to buy a nude drawing she had made in class! He'd seen it on the bulletin board of the classroom, found out who she was, and paid her $25 for it. She hadn't actually been paid for anything since her days at R. H. White's. The thrill this gave her was so huge she didn't dare admit it to anyone.

Being paid. "Meaningful work." It may have been only $25 but it meant that someone had taken something she had done seriously; something she had done outside her domestic life. It gave her hope that others might too. Finally Kate was ready to take her mother's advice and "pull herself together."

She let herself daydream about what to do next. The daydreaming led her back to the playroom basement and the books she had read there. She thought about her long-ago conversation with Ian about the brass head and his asking her if she liked science. And telling him about throwing salts in the Bunsen burner. How beautiful the colors were! And Ian and geology.

The daydreaming led her to think about making a children's book, a children's book about science. She began to plan. She bought herself an array of expensive watercolor tubes, Winsor Newton from England, and the best Arches watercolor paper, 190-lb. rough. (She loved it that the Arches Company had been founded in 1492, the year Columbus set sail, and the year her favorite artist, Piero della Francesca, died.)

She carried home histories of science from the library and she quizzed Jim's science friends to help her understand ideas she had. Some of the professors were amused, some were encouraging, some scoffed. She paid no attention to the last. She conjured up a schedule and she stuck to it. More or less. At least when the plumber wasn't there or the cleaning lady or a sick child.

It wasn't the life of glamour and adventure she had once envisioned but it satisfied her for now and turned her days into something resembling a real job. And the brilliant wet colors spreading into each other as though they were following some strange alchemy delighted her more than she could have believed.

Kate felt a new appreciation of herself, and this appreciation permeated her life. Jim noticed. "You're looking good these days, kiddo," he would say, and he wanted to make love more.

Sometimes before stepping into a hot bath now she would stop in front of the full-length mirror. Sucking in her stomach and pulling her shoulders back and down she would survey herself. Not so bad really even now after two children, certainly better than some of those models they drew.

She fantasized about having an affair and then abruptly shut the thought away. Besides, with whom would she have it? One of Jim's colleagues? The mailman? More importantly, she loved her husband. He really couldn't have been a better husband.

Jim Morse, as a tenured professor and role model to the young, didn't ride bicycles into lakes any more but he could still be jolly and carefree. Everyone liked him. His hair turned white and shaggy and he sprouted a beard to match. Freckled and smiling, as his waistline expanded and his face softened he grew both figuratively and literally into the best kind of academic. He wore rumpled tweeds and baggy trousers but, unlike some of his more pretentious colleagues, he couldn't give less of a damn about fine wines or renting vacation villas in Umbria.

Good beer, good scotch, and good talk with well-told jokes were his specialties. He loved parties and he was a terrific host.

"Hey, have a beer. You have time for a beer. Or two or three." Or "Join us for dinner," he would bark, clapping someone on the back. "Katie won't mind. Always room for one more." No one could pass their threshold without being made to feel at home.

James Joyce had become another specialty of his and he

took over organizing Bloomsday every June sixteenth after old Professor Ambleside was felled by a stroke.

As the original *Ulysses* readers succumbed to various geriatric impediments Jim gathered up other suitable people he could typecast into reading parts. When the Latin teacher Phillipa Pettit retired and went to live with her daughter in Utah he talked Kate into being Gerty MacDowell. Kate would have loved to read Molly but that role always went to plump Lizbet Gilligan, she of the low-cut peasant blouses, volcanic gray hair, and Comparative Pre-Christian Mythologies.

So every year around June fourteenth Kate prepared by rereading the pages about the three girls and the three children on the Dublin beach. And every year it reminded her of that day Ian came to see her at Burnmouth and they began their love affair on Tattoo Island.

CHAPTER 17

THE BIRTHDAY PARTY

The trouble in civilised life with entertaining company, as it is called too generally without much regard to its strict veracity, is so great that it cannot but be matter of wonder that people are so fond of attempting it. It is difficult to ascertain what is the quid pro quo.
Anthony Trollope, *Barchester Towers*

People who live all year in the country are not troubled with formal dinner giving, because (excepting on great estates) formality and the country do not go together, and to the house of limited equipment formal dinners are not to be thought of.
Emily Post, *Etiquette*

When Jim was about to turn thirty-nine they decided to celebrate this birthday instead of waiting for his fortieth. It seemed so trite to celebrate the fortieth like everyone else, and besides it was time they "paid back" a lot of people who had had them to parties. At least this was what Kate told Jim, but really she just felt the need for a party. They invited all the *Ulysses* readers as well as scores of other professors, graduate students, post-docs, graduates, and anybody Jim ran into in the street.

"God knows how we will ever fit them all in," said Kate.

She was happy for a project that she knew something about, for which she had actually been raised, been groomed, and she threw herself into an obsession of planning.

"Card tables," Katie enthused to Jim. "We can rent or borrow card tables and those pretty gold chairs and put them all over the house. Then we can seat people and it won't be like those faculty events where the men and women go off separately."

"People don't want to be told where to sit," countered Jim. "Let them wander around, find whom they want to plunge into profound discussions with." He could feel a marital storm brewing.

"We can have the men switch at dessert the way Mrs. White used to do."

"When people are deep in conversation you're going to snatch them away?! Listen, Kate, this isn't the social scene of your youth. Don't try to control people."

"But you need to control people. Parties are social engineering! No, they're even more, they're works of art, performance art!"

"Performance art? We'll make people take off their clothes and stand on their heads!"

Kate didn't laugh. She was thinking about the social scene of her youth and perhaps for the first time it struck her how serious all that triviality had been. Entertaining had been the "meaningful work" of people like her grandmother, her mother, and their female friends, as much as making money had supposedly been the work of men. This division of labor caused their world to prosper.

Parties were where people formed alliances, started flirtations, love affairs; they were where the old taught their formalities, their manners, to the young. She felt strongly about all this but it was so hard to explain.

Jim was wandering away and she followed him.

"No one should ever consider parties trivial. Parties celebrate traditions. And they celebrate good things: delicious food, drink, and conversation, and flowers that remind people of happy summers and beautiful places." She took a deep breath. "Parties distract people from thoughts of death and disaster."

"Oh, give me a break," said Jim, turning around and pinching her nose. Then he called to the dogs to go for a walk.

Of course social life in their college town was different from that of her mother and grandmother and Mrs. Andover White. First of all, there were no servants, no big houses, no big money. When people went to eat at other peoples' houses they brought bottles of wine, homemade cookies, supermarket bouquets in cellophane that you had to find a vase for; in season, a prize heirloom vegetable or two, before Christmas, a tree ornament.

Nor were caterers in profusion in northern New Hampshire, and there was nowhere within a hundred miles where you could rent tables, linens, and little gold chairs. Nor were there clubs to borrow them from. Eventually Kate and Jim agreed to have a buffet, and a major marital disturbance was avoided.

Kate looked around at her house, their house that they loved; the house that she had worked so hard over, surrounding it with forsythia, boxwood, and cedar, painting the front door Happy Tomato red, which made it the cheeriest house on the block. She had painted the downstairs walls in off whites, and the upstairs pale corals, soft blues, and powdery greens as close as she could come to the bedrooms at Burnmouth. They had added bookshelves, at first around the fireplace, and then more in the dining room, but before long the books had overflowed their shelves. Now there were books everywhere, on the tables, on the floor, horizontal books on top of vertical books in the shelves. There were old family photographs in dusty ornate frames, more recent ones in simple plastic ones, and then the latest ones unframed and tilted against the framed photographs or stuck in the edges. Toys belonging to humans and dogs lay underfoot, behind chairs, under tables. Every time she hid the puppy's beloved headless bunny (she hadn't the heart to dispose of it altogether), the puppy would find it and deposit even more of its dirty cotton innards here and there.

The fireplace looked like a war zone with piles of ashes and bits of charred wood; they would have to stuff it with logs to hide all that because there was no time to clean it out properly. Philodendrons and spider plants trailed sickly pale green streamers, and some huge leaves of the rubber plant had turned yellow. The fiddle leaf looked unhappy, and for the first time she noticed that tiny star blossoms from the Hoya had never been cleaned up from last summer and were sprinkled black and sticky over the windowsill. Though she thought she tended her plants lovingly, this was the middle of winter and the lushness of summer was six months away.

And the curtains! She hadn't given them a thought for years; no, it had been years since they'd been cleaned. The mats under the oriental rugs were showing like dirty underwear and dog hairs festooned the pillows.

As for the kitchen, not only the refrigerator but the toaster and the coffee maker, too, were galleries for children's drawings, postcards, and snapshots.

There was so much stuff. Stuff everywhere. Not to mention smudges! Smudges everywhere. Clutter everywhere. They had lived in the house less than a dozen years but had outgrown it not long after moving in.

Kate put aside her watercolor paintings for a while, propping them up on the washing machine and dryer in the small but sunny room off the kitchen, where they made a rather nice little art show. None was finished but they were bright and happy looking. Maybe they were actually better unfinished. Then she went to work on a project she considered equally artistic: getting her house ready for the party: cleaning, patching, painting, pruning, and hiding things in the basement.

"You are really something," laughed Jim, observing her manic activity. "You're knocking yourself out for a bunch of people who won't even notice and wouldn't care if they did!"

"It's the principle of the thing," answered Kate, and she realized it was exactly what her mother used to say.

The day of the party it snowed. Ten inches were predicted. Some people called in the late afternoon and said they couldn't get their cars started. After all, not all the people in a northern New England college town are northern New Englanders.

Katie, fluttering around the house, plumping pillows, angling books, removing wilted flowers from their arrangements, hadn't left herself much time to dress. How typical, she thought, not to have started earlier. She felt strongly that the good looks and charm of the hostess were the most important element of any party, and so she had thought for weeks about what to wear. Yet she hadn't even left herself enough time to try on the two or three outfits that were in the running.

The old claw-footed bathtub took forever to fill. Its tannish water dribbled out of the narrow spout and filled the bathroom with steam. That would mean frizzy hair. Never mind. Her curls would just be curlier than ever. She couldn't find the shoes she wanted and she threw all the possible pants and skirts and blouses on the bed in a colorful heap.

How much of her life had been spent preparing for parties, she thought. Even now. Pinning bra straps, buckling sandals, putting on panty hose with her rings turned around so as not to rip the nylon. Finding the right earrings. These panicked moments belonged to that earlier world when parties were the appreciated work of women of her class. No wonder the heroines of eighteenth-and nineteenth-century novels had maids to dress them.

When the first guests arrived Kate, as usual, wasn't ready. Why did their academic friends always come on time or even early?

Most of the guests removed their footwear in the "mudroom" and a big mountain of boots and shoes arose from a small lake of slush. Kate's elegant evening became a gathering of stocking feet. The children, who had looked forward to the party almost more than she had, were dressed in their best clothes. Nessa had been allowed to wear the slightly too big black velvet dress with lace collar Nancy had given her for Christmas, and Jamie's first bow tie had tiny lobsters on it. He clearly knew how good he looked in his navy blue blazer and tie. Their faces flushed with excitement, they carried the wet coats, scarves, and hats into the guest room. Twin peaks soon rose on the twin beds, and as happens with all mountains, erosion occurred. Garments tumbled to the floor, delighting the Irish setters, who circled around in them when they weren't obliged to bark at the doorbell. A distinguished law professor (he had been at the Nuremburg trials) deposited his coat, fur hat, and leather gloves in the bedroom's wastebasket. He explained to the children that years of experience had taught him this was the only way to find them afterwards.

Upstairs, Kate was still pawing through her choices, finally opting for the most inappropriate clothes from her own mountain, a pair of burgundy velvet slacks, a bit too tight, and a sparkly black top, cut a bit too low. She threw the rest of the clothes into the floor of her closet. Not being able to find the shoes she wanted she squeezed into high-heeled gold sandals—which meant she had to remove the panty hose she'd put on, which meant not only would she freeze, but her imperfect pedicure would show. Granny McAllister's diamond bracelet and diamond earrings completed what she hoped and also feared was a very New York look. She floated downstairs into a collection of women in tweed trousers, Icelandic sweaters, and sack-like dresses from Laura Ashley. Only the men over seventy-five wore ties. Beards and eyeglasses everywhere.

Kate, a hummingbird among pigeons and owls, flitted about, interrupting discussions of tenure tracks and administrative missteps, and introducing people, sometimes forgetting their names. She should have been so good at this and yet she found herself occasionally stammering and even shaking. Sometimes she had to lean over to greet people who were seated on the floor and didn't struggle to get up. With her left hand she tried to shelter her décolletage. She passed platters of cheeses and crackers, and raw vegetables with her special dip. The children passed bowls of nuts. This would have been a good time to have had a caterer and charming hors d'oeuvres, because as she'd told Ian years ago, she couldn't follow recipes. It had been traumatic enough to attempt the curry.

She found Heather Anderson seated in the lotus position on the floor of a corner of the living room, one arm around an Irish setter. Kate was squatting next to her when Jim arrived with two plates heaped with food and lowered himself down next to them. He handed one plate to Heather and dove into the other himself.

An odd sense of something crossed Kate's mind. Surely it couldn't be jealousy. Dear Heather, and dear Jim. Of course he was just being a good host to her good friend. Of course he was.

But she checked a bit later, having made her rounds twice, and saw that they seemed almost oblivious to the others, so engrossed were they in a discussion of Heidegger. Jim was doing the talking, Heather's soft eyes on his.

Heidegger. And her husband and best friend weren't the only ones discussing philosophy and other deep subjects. In her flutterings around the rooms she caught snatches of conversations that made her realize, not for the first time, that she was an outsider in this group. She knew literature of course, she was a reader, but philosophy, science, mathematics, linguistics, the professional pursuits of these people existed in a different realm from her happy amateurism.

When finally Kate felt people had had enough to eat and drink she gathered a pile of dirty dishes, left them next to the kitchen sink and retreated to her laundry/painting room in search of some solitary gulps of wine and a few deep breaths. There she found Lizbet Gilligan smoking with a man she had never seen before.

"Kate, dear, did you meet Lionel Rubin, my agent friend from New York?"

Kate couldn't remember Lizbet asking if she could bring anyone.

"We both love your paintings." Lizbet waved a hand heavy with Santa Fe jewelry in the direction of the yellow-orange suns, red-purple explosions, and sparkly stars on vivid blue backgrounds; Kate's watercolor universe.

"They're quite marvelous," said Lionel Rubin. "Have you ever considered doing a children's book?"

CHAPTER 18

STIRRING PITCHBLENDE

Never had [she] looked prettier than she did now. It was an undefinable loveliness that comes from joy, enthusiasm, and success; from a harmony of temperament and circumstances. Her ever-youthful illusions had the same effect as compost, rain, wind and sun on a flower, developing her by degrees, and she was finally blooming in the fullness of her nature.
Gustave Flaubert, *Madame Bovary*

I just want my own lemonade back," said Zack in a plaintive voice on the telephone.

"I know. Poor Daddy."

No matter how many tests they did at Mass General, they couldn't find out what was wrong with Zack, why he felt so awful, why there was blood in his urine. In the end, it was one of the summer doctors who had come up with the diagnosis. Zack was still at Burnmouth at the end of September when Kate called the town physician, Dr. Goodworthy, the one they had used only for poison ivy, rusty nails, and sprained ankles all these years. She knew that Zack had consulted him after the Mass General tests had been inconclusive. It must have given the small town doctor a perverse pleasure to say, "I don't care what the fancy Harvard doctors say, it's clear to me that your father has pancreatic cancer."

So in October it was decided to go to a really good medical center in New York and see if there was anything that could be done.

When Katie arrived from New Hampshire she took a taxi from the Port Authority bus station straight to Zack's hospital. Poor Zack, he looked as though he'd been run over by a truck. He was wearing a pale blue hospital gown with what looked like little flowers on it, and what was left of his lovely dark hair, now flecked with gray, was matted and damp. His pale face had purple sores, his lips were purple too, and the whites of his eyes were yellow. He reached a shaking arm out to her when she sat down next to him.

"K-K-K-Katie," he sputtered. And then he was trying to sing, "The most beautiful girl in the world isn't Garbo, isn't Grable...."

The words sounded as though they were coming from the old Victrola in their childhood playroom when it needed rewinding. He kept his hand in hers until it seemed to drop of its own accord, then he turned away and paid no more attention to her. Or to anything else.

"You do look beautiful, Katie dear," said Nancy, as always trying to save a social situation. "Better than you have in years. I think having your book published has been a real tonic for you."

Amidst the beeping contraptions in the hot room with its layers of falsely sweet smells, Nancy and Kate tried to cheer each other up. Kate gave her reports on Nessa, Jamie, and Jim, and her bus ride from New Hampshire. Kate embroidered each answer with as much interesting detail as possible, as though trying to bring the fresh air of New England into this terrible place. Occasionally Zack would groan and Kate wondered how much he heard or understood.

Kate had come to New York to be with her mother as well as her father. She hated leaving her kids at Halloween, their favorite holiday, but Zack was dying of what had finally been confirmed as pancreatic cancer. Even though Carrie lived in New York, she was busy running an art gallery and didn't have a lot of time to provide the help and companionship Nancy needed. Zack needed Kate too, she supposed, and, yes, she needed him.

She planned to comfort Nancy and cook for her in the little apartment a friend had lent them, and she would spell Nancy beside the deathbed.

The apartment they were borrowing was tiny but charming. The kitchen was minuscule, as was the only bathroom, but the building was old, the ceilings high, and the mullioned windows looked out on other charming buildings. There was even a real fireplace. On the round dining table the curvilinear stems of little pumpkins pointed in various directions as though searching for extraterrestrial life. There was one bedroom, which Kate insisted Nancy have to herself; Kate would sleep on the couch in the living/dining room.

One bright light in this gloomy trip to New York was that Kate was going to meet with the publisher Lionel Rubin had found for her. Imagine, her own publisher! The book she had illustrated and written (with help from Jim's scientific colleagues) was actually going to be published.

It was an exuberant book for the two-to-six age group with bright double-page illustrations of big moments in the history of science. Some of the moments might have actually happened. There was Archimedes jumping out of his bathtub, running wet and naked down the street yelling "Eureka, eureka!" He was also seen setting the Persian fleet afire with a magnifying glass. There was Isaac Newton in an orchard examining the apple that had fallen on his head; Darwin contemplating earthworms; Marie Curie stirring huge cauldrons of pitchblende from the Carpathian Mountains to extract radium; and two Einsteins, a big one and a little one inside the big one's thought bubble, falling in an elevator. She hadn't left out Friar Roger Bacon and his exploding brass head, though she wasn't sure that was actually science; she hoped her editor wouldn't remove him. Her idea was that if children loved and remembered these pictures, then later they would be curious when they came across the correct information. She was very proud of her book, it had taken years to produce, and the idea that it was really going to be published had energized her enormously.

Though she was in her late thirties now, she had never looked lovelier, and it was not only her mother who said so. She believed it to be true because, at last, she felt great. She had finally accomplished something in her life, if only a children's book. She had a good marriage and two wonderful children. She lived in a beautiful place. She was sure even her sometimes-difficult relationship with her adolescent son would survive with flying colors.

Little Jamie had changed recently. His voice had started cracking and pimples sprouted on his forehead. He had let his hair grow so that he looked like a member of a rock band and sometimes he tied a faded bandanna or a piece of leather around his head. Often a strand of his blond hair hung in his face that he liked to blow out of his eyes from below. In spite of the slovenliness, he was beautiful, she thought. Yet he didn't really seem to belong to her and Jim anymore. A sullen new teenager had replaced the enthusiastic boy they had known.

Zack had been sick for so long she felt she had already mourned him. Or so she told herself. She couldn't get her mind around Zack's dying; deep inside she felt numb. Yet occasionally, from the very bottom of myriad layers of feeling she wasn't even aware of, a thought would float up and she would imagine herself saying to him, "Don't think you're going to spoil my hard-won success and happiness just because you're dying." And then she would be ashamed and try to convince herself that she had forgiven him for his possessiveness and jealousy, his behavior to Ian long ago.

She was happy that she would be with her mother, whom she loved and hadn't spent time with for years. Together in the tiny apartment they would have a chance to be close again while they waited.

Her first night in New York Carrie was coming to dinner, and Kate looked forward to seeing her sister. Their relationship would always be competitive, but Kate felt ready to take it on again.

"Katie, you look marvelous!" Carrie was using that voice they called "Long Island lockjaw." She came out of the birdcage elevator with her arms full of bags from Zabar's while Kate held back the iron accordion door. With her arms full Carrie couldn't return Kate's hug so Kate kissed her cheek and then took as many of the bags as she could and carried them to the kitchen. The sisters stood back and surveyed each other and Kate felt what she always felt. Carrie's hair was so beautiful! She had a short asymmetrical cut and her tailored black pantsuit set off her blondness like a jewel in a velvet box. And she was what Kate and her friends called "New York thin." Kate felt disheveled and dowdy in her blue jeans. Her hair was too long.

The next noon after Kate had done her shift beside Zack's hospital bed, she met Carrie for lunch at her club. It was in a lovely old Park Avenue building where a uniformed doorman opened the door under an anonymous canopy. The ladies' room was mirrored and enormous. Kate handed her hooded down coat to the attendant, wishing she'd had it cleaned before coming to New York. Then she tried to ignore her reflection as she combed her hair while around her stiffly groomed New York matrons poked at their lacquered coiffeurs and powdered their noses. Carrie arrived slightly breathless. She chatted and nodded to some of the other ladies, who all seemed happy to see her.

"What a morning!" exclaimed Carrie in her lockjaw voice. She had switched out of it last night as the sisters had begun to reminisce and giggle but now in the harsh light of day it was back again.

The sisters climbed to the dining room on an imposing staircase lined with paintings of equally imposing women. The costumes of these ladies began with nineteenth-century ruffles and ended with tailored Chanel suits. The sisters ate fish with a sauce so delicate and delicious it seemed made of perfume. They each had a glass of white wine. Carrie described the exhibition she was working on, how it would open in three days, the catalogue that she had written wasn't even back from the printer yet, what bad timing for their father to be sick right now!

Kate said nothing in return but she felt a twinge of schadenfreude that in their eternal competition, Carrie should seem the less caring of the two.

As Carrie wiggled into the coat the attendant held for her, she told Kate she'd walk with her as far as her gallery and then Kate could go on to the Whitney Museum. She thought a nice brisk walk would do her good. Particularly after that chocolate soufflé!

Carrie's coat was dark green wool with a black fur mandarin collar and cuffs. As she pulled on black leather gloves she gazed at Kate's puffy coat from L. L. Bean. They did not look like sisters as they started up Park Avenue.

"I must say," said Carrie, "I find her solicitude a bit suspect."

"Whose solicitude?" Kate had no idea what Carrie was talking about.

"Mother's, of course. Hanging out by his bedside like that day after day. I mean, does he even know she's there?"

"Of course he knows."

"She's coming around a little late, don't you think? Where was she all those years when he really needed her?"

"What are you talking about? It was our father who was off having affairs, not our mother."

"Doesn't that tell you something? That he needed to have affairs? Our mother is a cold woman."

"Carrie, please, let's not."

For several blocks they walked on silently. They turned off the expansiveness of Park Avenue and down a side street of elegant brownstones bordered by trees with spotted trunks. Kate loved those spotted trunks, they belonged in a children's book. She had tried to tell Carrie about her book but Carrie had been too preoccupied to say more than, "How nice for you."

"Let's face it," Carrie continued. "Our mother is a cold person and our childhood was a mess."

"I loved our childhood. My childhood."

"How often was our mother there for us? How often did she express any real love for us? Can you imagine how Daddy felt? He once told me he wished they didn't sleep in twin beds because they couldn't roll over and bump into each other in the night. Imagine! Only by bumping into your spouse by mistake might you have sex!"

"I thought Mummy was an excellent mother. Of course she had her faults, of course she got angry at us. I mean she wasn't perfect. You know how hard it is to be a parent. We both know that. Come on, Carrie."

But Carrie was a dog with a bone. They turned north on Madison Avenue, passing the smart stores with their haughty mannequins in beautiful clothes, mostly black. The Long Island lockjaw disappeared, replaced by the voice of an angry kid. Carrie wouldn't let go and Kate wouldn't agree with her. Kate heard the adolescent hurt in her sister's voice, the hurt that Carrie would probably feel for the rest of her life.

Carrie had had a lot of psychotherapy; perhaps this was where her outburst was coming from. Perhaps Carrie and her therapist had decided everything was their mother's fault. Kate was suspicious of psychotherapy, suspicious that it turned real people into fictional ones, real events into a connected narrative such as a writer would invent. She worried that it didn't correctly mirror the world.

That hopeless conversation with Carrie was one reason Kate decided to treat her mother to dinner on Halloween. She loved Halloween with its manic craziness and wanted to celebrate it. It was the one night of the year you could become a witch or a pumpkin—or a ghost, without dying. You could be anything you wanted. Most important, you could be a child again.

And Kate had read in the paper that this Halloween there would be a full moon, the second one of the month, a blue moon.

Kate made reservations for two at the Café des Artistes. The restaurant was just down the street from their apartment and Kate enjoyed walking by it. Its window boxes overflowed with autumn grasses, flowers, and vines, their subtle deterioration giving them a wistful elegance. That night Kate wore an expensive deep-coral-colored dress she had bought that morning at Bergdorf Goodman and her hair in a chignon (very soigné, said her mother). Carrie's style had shamed her into doing something about her own much-too-country look. Maybe the royalties would pay for the dress.

In the 1970s the Café des Artistes was one of the most beautiful restaurants in New York. There were plants and flowers everywhere, and painted nymphs floated naked across the walls. The little Art Nouveau lamps gave a flattering glow that almost made people forget they were not in Paris.

It was there that Kate, looking over her shoulder to study the mural of The Swing Girl, wondering if she might adapt the vine-swinging redheaded nymph for a children's book—that she saw Ian.

He was with a group of people and his back was to her. At first she wasn't sure and then, straining, she was able to hear his voice. Even though his group was speaking French, she became more and more convinced that it was he.

"Mother, don't turn around—no, please don't turn around! I think that's Ian over there in the corner."

"Ian?"

"You remember Ian. The boy that Daddy threatened to kill. We ran off to Princeton and you made us sandwiches. Twenty years ago."

"Oh, of course. Are you going to speak to him?"

"I don't know."

Kate stole glances at Ian's table. Four men, all very well dressed. Two women, about the same age, also well dressed. Extremely chic actually. All in black. Was one Ian's wife? Kate tried to eat a mouthful of salad but her hand was shaking and a piece of watercress fell off the fork. She put the fork down and sighed.

"That was hard on you, wasn't it Katie?"

But Kate wasn't listening to her mother.

"I don't know what to do."

"Perhaps if you wait they will pass our table on the way out and then you can see if it's really him."

"No, I bet they'll be here longer than we will. They're foreigners, they'll linger and talk forever."

"Then we'll linger and talk even longer. How about dessert? Or maybe another glass of wine."

"Both," said Kate, and her mother called the waiter over.

Ian got up from his table and headed for the men's room. Yes, it was definitely Ian, better looking than ever, prosperous looking.

"When he comes back from the men's room we'll be in his line of sight," said Katie. She sat up very straight, folded her hands in her lap and tried to breath smoothly.

"Katie, when he comes out, go to him. Don't let this pass by. You'd never forgive yourself."

So Kate stood up, and clutching her napkin in one hand, she went to stand outside the Ladies' Room door near to where he had to pass. Her legs were shaking, and she realized she must have looked ridiculous holding the big white napkin, but she took a deep breath and reminded herself that she was successful now, successful and beautiful, so when he came by she didn't hesitate to reach out and touch his forearm.

"Ian," she said in almost a whisper. "It's Katie."

"Katie."

He stopped and they looked at each other. And then came the smile, after all those years still his wonderful smile, and she returned her own. Waiters balancing their big trays were trying to get by them and when he held her elbow to guide her out of the way she felt it through her whole body.

"Where are you sitting?"

"Over there. With Mother."

"May I join you for a minute?"

"Of course."

She knew him well enough to know he was glad to see her. She had been terrified but also full of hope and now she knew it would be all right. Nancy told Kate afterward how beautiful she looked when she brought Ian to their table.

"You looked lovely to begin with, of course, but then you became just radiant. Oh, Katie, I think you're still in love with him."

Ian said he was in New York for a trade conference, something to do with mining, he and a colleague had just arrived from Ottawa and would be here for three days. They were dining with old friends, two couples who lived in Manhattan. He'd love to take Kate and her mother out for a nightcap. Nancy said it was a lovely idea but she thought she'd go back to the hospital for an hour or so and then to bed. Kate didn't need to join her and should certainly go along with Ian.

"I'd love to," said Kate.

After Ian had said goodbye to his friends and all the checks had been paid, Ian and Kate walked with Nancy to Central Park West where they found her a cab. Then they walked to a bar Ian knew near the Museum of Natural History. Miniature goblins and ghosts, ferocious furry animals, winsome fairies, and wicked witches zigzagged past them, running, jumping, yelling, squealing, attacking the buckets of candy doormen held out.

"Kids are such little optimists, so delighted with everything," said Katie. For a second Jamie and Nessa flashed across her mind. Nessa was going to be Alice in Wonderland this year and Jamie, what was Jamie planning to be? She couldn't remember.

"They're scientists, they're busy figuring out how things work."

"Exactly!" she said, then hesitated for a moment.

"I've written a book about science for kids!" she blurted out.

"That's wonderful. I want to hear about it. About everything."

It was dark and quiet in the underground bar. They sat at a copper table in a corner and she ordered a White Russian—the kind of drink she hadn't ordered in years. He ordered cognac.

"So you've written a book. Tell me about it."

"Oh no, I didn't mean to talk about it. It's nothing. A children's book. It was just that seeing those kids, their enthusiasm..."

He reached for her hand where it lay on the table. She jumped. That smile again.

"You're still so diffident. I'd love to hear about the book. Tell me."

So she told him about the book.

"Louis Agassiz and his Ice Age? Do you have Agassiz and his *époque glaciare*?

"I don't. I'm sorry."

"That would be wonderful, a fat Frenchman about to be inundated by an avalanche of ice. Covering half the globe!"

"The closest thing to geology is Madame Curie stirring pitch-blende from the Carpathian Mountains."

He laughed. "That counts!"

"I'll put Monsieur Agassiz in the sequel."

"What a great idea—to make children love science before they know it's supposed to bore them."

"I couldn't resist putting Friar Bacon's brass head in. Even though that really wasn't science."

"Perhaps the brass head was only legend but Roger Bacon, also known as Doctor Mirabilis, was enormously important. In fact many consider him, rather than Francis Bacon, to be the father of empiricism."

He brought her fingertips up to his lips.

"Time is, Time was...."

"Don't explode!" she laughed.

"Not here," he said, "not yet."

She felt herself blushing and retrieved her hand so she could take another sip of the very full White Russian cocktail.

"Diffident still, but different. Your posture, your movements are different. You've become a beautiful woman of the world."

Woman of the world? She didn't know what to say.

"I'm sorry about your father being so ill. Is there hope?"

"No. It's just a matter of time. His heart is still so strong, it's taking forever. His body doesn't want to give up. Even though, even though...." No, she wasn't going to cry. Another sip while he waited. "Even though he isn't really there anymore. I don't think he even knows we're sitting beside him, Mummy and I. And Carrie comes when she can."

"That's so hard on you."

"It's no fun."

"You're a good daughter. I'm sure he knows you're there, you and your mother. I'm sure at some level he senses it."

"A good daughter?" Now she thought she really might cry after all. All those fights they'd had. All those political arguments that had turned personal. Yet she knew that her father loved her and she loved him. So much so that now it felt like a paralysis creeping inside her.

She surprised herself when she said, "He was awful to you that night."

At first Ian seemed surprised too, maybe shocked, then he smiled at her.

"No one had ever threatened to kill me before."

He continued to smile and she understood the smile as an invitation to go further. And partly because of the lovely vodka, Kahlua, and cream, she did.

"Of course he wouldn't have killed you, he was just such a baby, he was so jealous. Or something."

What she really wanted to ask was if that was why he, Ian, had left her. Was it only because of her father? But she wasn't ready to ask and they both knew it was time to change the subject.

"Twenty years," he said. "Think of all that's happened to the world since we last saw each other."

"The Viet Nam War."

"The assassinations of the Kennedys."

"And Martin Luther King. The civil rights movement."

"Woodstock. Berkeley."

"Hippies and the Beatles."

"The discovery of plate tectonics."

And The Pill and the sexual revolution, she wanted to say

but didn't. And panty hose, replacing girdles and garter belts. She hoped it was too dark for him to see how red her face was. But he noticed.

"Katie, Katie, Katie," he said.

They sat silently for a while and then she said, "You're married, aren't you?"

It was Zack who had shown her, three or four years after he had threatened to kill Ian, that issue of *Town and Country*, rolled open to the page where the photograph and announcement were. Was it an apologetic expression on Zack's face as he handed it to her? A complicated expression, in any case. She had taken the magazine and studied the picture of the Canadian mining-fortune heir and the cabinet minister's daughter. The bride was beautiful, serene, a little taller than Ian. She wore a very simple dress, almost like a satin slip, and held a bouquet of white calla lilies.

"Yes, and I have three children. And you're married too, you wear a ring."

"Yes."

"Children?"

"A boy almost fifteen and a girl twelve."

"None of which will prevent me from taking you to the Metropolitan Museum tomorrow as soon as I can duck out of the meetings. And to dinner afterward, I hope."

"I would love that."

And so began three days of visits to museums, walks in the park, a chamber music concert, and when there was no one they could possibly know around, hand holding. The last leaves were falling in Central Park, but some brave bushes still blazed yellow and red; a soft autumn light sparkled through the filigree of naked branches.

One afternoon they found a quiet bench in the park not far from the reservoir. There were a few toddlers trying to escape from their nannies and an occasional sniffing dog went by pulling someone on a leash, but mostly they were alone. It felt to Kate that the time had come to talk about that odd incident at the end of their first love affair. They had become close enough.

"I've thought about it so often. Why Daddy acted that way. I decided there were lots of reasons."

"You tell me your analysis and I'll tell you mine."

"Well, first, he was jealous of you. You were young and obviously going to be successful, while he had squandered so much talent and money that we had to live in that horrible house."

Ian's expression didn't change.

"And he was jealous because not only I liked you, but Mummy obviously did too. And also you'd taken me away from the Chicago coming-out parties. He really wanted me to find someone...."

She hesitated, not knowing quite how to put it.

He helped her out.

"Someone you all knew. Someone more from your social set, as they say. Not some exotic interloper from across the border!" He was laughing.

She couldn't tell him her father had called him a wog.

"What do you think his problem was?"

"I think he couldn't stand the thought of his beloved daughter in the arms of another man."

He changed his plane ticket, stayed over one more day. Their last night while Nancy was at the hospital they were having a glass of wine in the borrowed apartment when he took her in his arms.

"I know you've read *Gatsby*," he said.

She nodded.

"Do you remember that part toward the end of the book, he's describing their last afternoon together before he went in the army."

"Let me think a minute." So she thought, feeling sad in a lovely way, and then it came back to her and she could almost quote it. "Yes, there was a fire in the room. Wasn't it November like now? He was holding her and they were so quiet...."

"'The afternoon had made them tranquil....as if to give them a deep memory for the long parting....'"

He had begun to kiss her, really kiss her for the first time in years, when the phone rang. She almost didn't answer, but then she knew she had to.

"It's over," said Nancy's voice.

Between saying goodbye to her father's body and helping Nancy and Carrie make the arrangements to send it back to Maine for the funeral, and then arranging the funeral itself, Kate had a chance to duck into a little bookstore on Columbus Avenue and buy herself a copy of *The Great Gatsby*. Hardly a comforting book, but she read it over and over, as though it were a prayer book that would help her get her through this difficult time:

On the last evening afternoon before he went abroad, he sat with Daisy in his arms for a long silent time. It was a cold fall day, with fire in the room and her cheeks flushed. Now and then she moved and he changed his arm a little, and once he kissed her dark shining hair. The afternoon had made them tranquil for a while, as if to give them a deep memory for the long parting the next day promised.

Kate and Nancy took the train to Boston, where Jim and the children met them, and then they all drove up the chilly coast of Maine, now unwelcoming in its bleak beauty. Nancy had insisted they could manage at Burnmouth, though it wasn't a winter house and it had already been closed against the cold. Obviously Nancy hadn't money to spend on a hotel and she knew Jim didn't have much either. But still. A few nights in a hotel? Maybe it was something else that made her want to bring her family back to Burnmouth in almost freezing weather. Carrie and her family stayed at the new Bar Harbor Motor Inn.

Kate moved in a daze. The two amazing happenings, her father's death and the return of her old love, had unsettled her. After the funeral she returned with her family to New Hampshire, where everything looked the same but was now irrevocably different. When Bloomsday came the following June she told Jim she felt sick and to please find someone else to read Gerty MacDowell.

CHAPTER 19

LES ROCHERS CAPRICIEUX

We do not go, we are carried along like things that float, now gently, now with violence, depending on whether the water is angry or serene.
Michel de Montaigne, "On the Inconsistency of our Actions"

At night we were stained by dew and shamed into pettiness by the innumerable silences of stars.
T. E. Lawrence, *Seven Pillars of Wisdom*

Kate decided to try out her French on the taxi driver. Her poor miserable French that she had taken for years (twelve, was it?) and had still managed to fail her sophomore year. She just couldn't pay attention in her school days. She had heard that the Canadians were more relaxed about their native tongue than the real French and besides, if she had dared to come here to Montreal she could dare anything.

"*Merci beaucoup,*" she said to the driver as she handed him the odd-looking dollars, and when he handed change back, she said, "*Non, pour vous.*"

The narrow stone building on the Rue de la Commune must once have been a warehouse, or some sort of commercial building in any case. It was only four or five stories tall, and the double rows of windows were set off with boxes of red geraniums. As she dragged her luggage to the front steps, she felt she was entering a fairy tale, or perhaps a jigsaw puzzle.

A boy in a striped vest and bow tie appeared out of nowhere and took her suitcase.

"*Bon soir, bon soir, Madame,*" he said, leading her to the reception desk. The walls of the dim lobby, lit only by a wrought-iron chandelier with several of its bulbs out, were exposed brick. The furniture was covered in a purple-and-brown flowered print. She couldn't take it all in right away but soon she understood that the hotel was a charming combination of nineteenth-century mercantile, roughhewn stone, and contemporary chic. Perfect.

Upstairs, an envelope rested on the brass tray beside the bed. "I will meet you at Les Rochers Capricieux at eight. Ian." His note gave an address and directions but nothing else. As though he didn't want to leave incriminating evidence.

She was disappointed but glad at the same time. She would have time to bathe and dress and "pull herself together," as her mother would say. What would Nancy think if she knew about this? Somehow, she thought, or convinced herself, that Nancy wouldn't have minded. Too much. She hadn't minded about the mud on the dress that day of the ferry dock. And hadn't she been the one who urged Kate to speak to Ian in New York? She could hear her mother saying, "I just want you to be happy, precious."

Kate unpacked the dark red dress and hung it in the bathroom so that the steam would smooth it. It was not so different from the black one of the garden party years ago, except instead of those silly puffed sleeves, the fabric hugged the arms all the way to the wrist. Then she stood at the window and looked out over the geraniums. The sidewalk underneath swarmed with activity: smiling couples of all ages walked hand in hand and sometimes stopped to kiss, children lapped ice cream cones, young people leaned against parked cars and motorcycles, dogs strained on leashes. Across the busy traffic, and past swaths of park, lay the broad St. Lawrence, its edges clogged with boats of all sizes. The large, generous river seemed to think it was an ocean, making Boston, less than two hours away, seem part of a different continent. Someone was playing an accordion. And there was a competing melody, piercing but more delicate, yes, someone else was playing a violin. Was it *"Plaisir d'Amour?"*

She felt forgiven before she had even sinned. This was a city that believed in love.

The restaurant, like the cobblestoned streets that led to it, like the hotel she had walked from, like all of this Vieux Port of Montreal, seemed built on a child's scale. She ducked into the candlelit vestibule, which smelled of garlic and browned butter, and before the maitre d' had a chance to greet her, she saw Ian. He rose from the table and came toward her. He wore a crisp suit and a silk tie and she noticed that his hair was not so dark as it had been even less than a year ago. He took her hands, kissed them both, kissed her forehead, and led her to their table. It was in an alcove and he pulled the chair that was against the window out for her. It was perfect; so far everything was perfect: the city, the hotel, the streets, the restaurant, the table, the flowers on the table, everything was perfect.

And yet she was terrified. She sat very straight and hoped the low neck of her dress was symmetrical, not sliding over to one side as the necks of her dresses often did. She smiled and tried to be calm. In her lap her hands were shaking.

"You look beautiful but scared," he said.

"I am scared," she said.

"Some wine," he said. "Some champagne, then you'll feel better."

"Actually, I feel wonderful."

Just don't let me mess this up, she thought.

The meal was perfect, too, but she didn't dare eat much. The weeks before this she had worried about her body, exercised more than usual and had even lost weight. A few nibbles of the turbot and a bit of salad (she hoped there wasn't too much garlic in the dressing) were enough. And, of course, the champagne. They talked about many things, the problem of French anger against the rest of Canada, tourism, Viet Nam. They talked about everything except what they were feeling.

In the elevator to her room she felt moist between her legs. Aching. She handed over the key and he let them in. Light from the street lamp fell on the bed and he sat down first and then patted the bed beside him. They faced each other, side by side, and he smiled. That same smile, the same smile she remembered from the Criterion movie theatre, so many years ago, just before the curtains with the weeping willows became transparent, just before they pulled apart.

Yes, she thought, this is what I am being faithful to, that time when I was fifteen. Nothing can ever be more important than that time, that moment and this one, its culmination. This silly thought, a thought that only a silly girl might have, made her smile. He took her chin in his hand and they were locked together in their smiles for a long moment. Then he kissed her eyes shut and slid the fingers of his other hand down her face, down her neck, over her collarbone and onto one breast. He moved the other hand too, slid her dress off her shoulder, and reached inside. It was a gentle exploration, making up for decades.

The sun woke her against his chest, her hand in its fur. She lay very still, entangled in the sheets and the odors of their intimacy. She lay there for a long time, her breathing a part of his breathing, unbelievably happy. All the rest of her life—her life at home, her family, her history—was shut out. Nothing before last night mattered. She had no idea what time it was.

When he awoke he kissed her.

"I want to take you somewhere today," he told her, "a place that may surprise you."

"I love surprises," she said.

They breakfasted in the restaurant below the lobby. It seemed a cave cut into the rock, dark with only little rectangles of bright morning peeking in the high windows. A fluffy woman in an enormous apron served them omelets aux fines herbes, café au lait, and croissants. Kate wished she had a sweater slung over her shoulders; she was cold in her bush jacket, the kind TV people wear on exotic assignments, open over a low-cut camisole. Ian wore a heavy black turtleneck and jeans. As usual she couldn't believe how good-looking he was. Much better looking than she, though she knew she was beautiful too, beautiful as good-looking women are after being made love to.

They drove east toward Quebec City and then beyond. Eventually they came to gently hilly country, curving lanes, fields of sunflowers. They passed houses like those in children's stories with peaked roofs and bright red and blue painted trim, shutters, and window boxes, happy little gardens, and frilly fences. The road bordered woods, rivers, and streams and, farther still, the great sea of the St. Lawrence appeared again and again. Finally they turned onto a road that sloped down toward the river, and then turned again between battered twin stone sculptures of lions into a long driveway. They stopped at the front of a large fieldstone house enhanced with pale green shutters, set in overgrown weeds. It seemed deserted until a thin man in jeans with tousled gray-flecked hair rushed to open her car door.

"*Monsieur, Madame,* Lady, hallo, hallo. *Bienvenue.* Velcome!" he sputtered at them. His grin was missing a tooth or two. He took their luggage and rushed inside with it, then disappeared up a grand staircase. Kate was aware of Ian watching her face as she surveyed the large hall, the huge vases of sunflowers, the French doors, through which she could see the river beyond.

"This is my Burnmouth," he said.

She insisted on a tour immediately. He took her hand and led her to a large living room with soft chairs and sofas slip-covered in faded linen roses, a dining room with painted blue furniture and pottery-filled cabinets (each room had its own fireplace), a wooden pantry leading to a utilitarian kitchen. The library seemed almost a cliché, an homage to all libraries in movies and literature, a sanctuary guarded by walls of books, a polar bear skin splayed out in front of the fireplace. She examined some of the titles that stretched to the ceiling. There were many volumes in French. He took one out and blew the dust off it. It was leather with gold-tipped pages.

"My grandfather's passion," he said. "He was always searching for lost time."

"Really? Your grandfather loved Proust?"

"My mother's parents were French. French from France. Brought up in Paris. Her father came to this country as a young man, built up a wine-importing business, became the largest wine importer in French Canada."

"Oh, Ian, I'm so ashamed. I've asked you so little about your family. I thought your family was Scottish, Scottish and of course Canadian."

"My father yes, his family was originally from Glasgow, and we were—still are—in mining, but my mother's family was French..." he paused, smiling, "French and Jewish."

"Like Proust," she said. Her father had said he was a wog. Perhaps what he had really wanted to say was "kike."

If it weren't for the late afternoon sun lighting the lovely landscape outside, she thought she could stay happily and then die happily in this wonderful room. It was there in the library that they would make love later. They both knew it as they stood there, and he kissed her forehead in acknowledgement.

The French doors opened on a terrace sheltered by tall cedars where weeds were struggling up between the flagstones and the iron furniture was rusty in places. Between the terrace and the faraway river lay windswept fields dotted with bushes and clumps of trees. No other houses were visible. The river had a landscape of its own, the islands looked surreal, as though they had been pulled and stretched, and the opposite shore was invisible. What a wonderful place to draw, she thought.

"There are whales in those waters," said Ian.

"And silkies?"

"Yes, silkies, absolutely." And he kissed her forehead again.

Louis-Marie was the name of the eager servant who had greeted them. Now he brought them steaming bowls of corn chowder, a baguette, and a bottle of white wine. He seemed to be the only other person around and he acted delighted to have them to wait on. Ian explained that Louis-Marie was the last of the staff that had worked for the family when Ian's parents were alive. Yet he was all that was needed because he could do everything: garden, fix things, clean the house, shop, tend the chickens, and cook delicious meals.

"Wait till tomorrow's breakfast, when you will experience his crepes."

The wine, the drive, and the lovemaking the night before made them sleepy. She could hardly remember last night, she had had much too much champagne. She retained at first only the aura of it, and then slowly some of the detail came back to her and she blushed.

Now, barely twelve hours afterward, without removing the quilt or their clothes they lay down on the large bed with their luggage, still packed, on the floor beside them. Lying in the crook of his arm she fell asleep immediately and dreamed puzzling dreams that, as they dissipated, left a sweet melancholy.

When the afternoon light began to dim they drove to a nearby village and attended a band concert. They sat on folding chairs outside a gazebo strung with little white lights as the sky reddened and then darkened and the local amateurs brought forth their own clumsy but passionate versions of Schubert, Saint Saëns, and ancient Quebecois folk songs. Aching again, Kate imagined the musicians were making love to their instruments.

After a delicious dinner of fish stew they carried their glasses of wine to the library where Louis-Marie had lit a fire. When he poked his head in to say good night, Louis-Marie's smile said that he was happy for them.

Ian turned off all but one lamp to supplement the firelight. She wondered if this was a concession to the vanity of a forty-year-old woman, but the warm soft glow was lovely and she was grateful.

This time his explorations were slower, more precise. Perhaps that was something learned over time, perhaps it was good that they had left behind the hurried enthusiasms of last night and before that of their youth. She wondered on how many women he had practiced his confident technique and this made him appeal to her even more.

Afterward they lay entwined on the leather sofa for a long time. She was amazed that he had never been inside her until last night. It was as though their love affair were a long, long foreplay, with the climax coming only now.

When the coals began to lose warmth he said, "Let's go count the stars." He took a dark blanket of green and blue plaid off the edge of the sofa and wrapped her in it.

"Jewish family tartan," he said. Huddled inside the soft cashmere and the strength of his arm she let herself be led out to the terrace. He rubbed her back to keep her warm.

"'The innumerable silences of stars,'" he said, looking up. Awestruck and shivering, they stood there as long as they could.

The coals in the tiled bedroom fireplace were mostly gray now, and the smell of the burning wood permeated the room. After they made love again they watched the remaining bits of light playing on the ceiling and whispered as though they weren't the only people for miles around.

"I wish...." He began.

"Yes, me too."

"You know what I'm thinking?"

"I hope so. I know what I'm thinking."

"I should have grabbed you when I could have. I should have ignored your father and carried you off like a medieval knight."

She loved that idea. The two heroes jousting over the delicate maiden. A story from one of the moldy old books in the Burnmouth playroom. But she knew that wasn't the real story. She knew she couldn't blame everything on her father.

Finally she dared ask the question whose answer she had wanted to know for years.

"Ian?"

"What, little Katie?"

"It wasn't just my father, was it? You had more or less tired of me before that, hadn't you?"

He moved slightly in the bed, putting his arms behind his head. He could have been counting the shadows on the ceiling.

"It was complicated. We were young. I was young and ambitious. I had plans that I was intent on carrying out. You were even younger. And you seemed a bit scatterbrained, rather fey—or perhaps unfocused is a better word. Which was your charm, of course. I worried how you would fit in."

"And there were other girls, weren't there?"

He brought his arms down and encircled her in them. He burrowed his face into the back of her turned away head.

"If I'd been able to see into the future....to see what you would become, the way you are now...."

But then there wouldn't have been Jamie and little Nessa. The sudden thought burst in and startled her. Jamie and Nessa's phantoms had joined them there in the dying firelight.

The next afternoon they drove back to Montreal in silence. She had spent the morning on the terrace sketching the landscape while he made some calls in the library. Then he had sat very still watching her while she drew him.

"Now I will know you in a different way," she said.

When she drew people she memorized unconsciously their features and their bone structure, even their expressions. Now, with Ian as her model, she felt more than ever the intimacy of drawing; the act seemed, more than ever, a kind of caressing. She never forgot a person she had drawn and now she had further reason to remember Ian forever.

He left the car with the porter and took her to her room. He apologized again for having to leave for Ottawa but his children and wife would be back from their weekend trip. She had known this, but she hadn't wanted to think about it.

Now she remembered all of it. She remembered the year of furtive planning, the secret post office box for letters, the phone calls from phone booths, the synchronization of dates, the lies to children and spouses. And finally Jim out of the country at the Conrad conference, her children with Nancy in Maine. Yet in spite of the care she took, she had noticed a funny look on Jamie's face recently, a look that made her worry. She wondered if her son, now flooded with his own new sexuality, and a particularly observant person to begin with, she wondered if he sensed what had happened to his mother. Did he know what she had done?

Ian wanted to pay for the dinner they wouldn't be able to have together, but she refused. She didn't really want to eat, she said; she might order something later from room service. They didn't go near the bed. They didn't even sit. They stood and he held her for a long time while she wept silently on his shoulder. He kissed the tears as they rolled down her cheeks.

"Hey," he said, as the tears came faster, "I can't keep up."

"Katie," he said, "I don't want this to be the last time. My family never comes to French Canada, they think it's too far and the kids get bored. I want you to join me here when you can."

"I would love that." She sniffled, they smiled at each other one last time, and then he left.

CHAPTER 20

JAMIE

Autumnal—nothing to do with leaves. It is to do with a certain brownness at the edges of the day.....Brown is creeping up on us, take my word for it....Russets and tangerine shades of old gold flushing the very outside edge of the senses...deep shining ochres, burnt umber and parchments of baked earth—reflecting on itself and through itself, filtering the light.
Tom Stoppard, *Rosencrantz & Guildenstern are Dead*

Jamie was alone in the house when she got back from the airport, lying on the sofa in the living room with the Sunday *New York Times* scattered about as though there had been a windstorm. She hadn't expected the children to return from Maine until later that night.

"I didn't feel good, so I came back early," he said. "I caught a ride with some friends."

"Oh." She was surprised, frightened. "What's wrong?"

"I don't know. I feel like shit. Probably mono."

She went to him and put out her hand to feel his forehead as though he were still little. He pushed it away.

"God," he said, "you smell like a forest fire. Where were you anyway?"

"Visiting," she said. "A friend."

"Oh. A friend." He turned over on the couch so that his back was to her and said into the pillows, "Don't tell me anymore."

At almost sixteen, Jamie was sullen, sophisticated, and unknowable. In just one short year he had changed from the funny, energetic, happy child with whom she had always felt so close. They had shared so many interests—they had both loved tales of exploration, they had skied and biked together, when she got a little tipsy from wine with dinner they would put on a record and Jamie, Nessa, the barking dogs, and she would dance around the dining room table. Not long ago she and Jamie had both dressed as pirates for Halloween, he as a swashbuckling hero, she as a toothless hag. Now he preferred to spend all his time with his daredevil friends, drinking beer probably, maybe even smoking pot, driving too fast probably, and though she knew some of that was normal, she worried.

She worried that she and Jamie had more in common than harmlessly exuberant interests. She hoped that he wasn't like she had been. Occasionally a vivid memory haunted her, and now one came hurtling back. Blurry headlights surprising pine trees, suddenly illuminating bushes mere inches away in the dark. She and Michael Blake and Tommy Brooke driving back from a party, all of them drunk. A policeman pulled them over in Somesville and made them get out of the car, the lights of his cruiser rotating on the empty night. He'd decided not to arrest them but ordered the boys not to drive. She would have to take the wheel, apparently because she was the girl, the responsible one. She remembered concentrating through the fog of her intoxication, guessing where underneath the car the crawling road might be, everyone's lives in her hands.

"Don't be the way I was," she wanted to tell Jamie. Did he know, she wondered, how drunk she had often been, how fast she had driven, how reckless she had been? How reckless she still was?

And she wondered if Nancy and Zack had known how close she had come to danger when she was Jamie's age. She had once loved the idea that she and Jamie were alike, but now as a parent it scared her.

"Don't ever call me "Chipmunk" again," he had said to her a few weeks ago when they were arguing about his curfew. It had been her pet nickname for him almost since he was born.

She went to get the thermometer, silently praying that she hadn't done something that would harm her family irrevocably.

He pulled his head out of the pillows.

"By the way, some dude called. Didn't speak good English, I think he was French. Something about your leaving a 'cahier.' A notebook, I guess. He said he would send it."

Of course, the sketchbook. Her heartbeat went wild. The book had her name, phone number, and address in the front written under "REWARD IF RETURNED." She must have left it on the terrace. Now she would have to be the first to go through the mail every day until the package arrived from Canada. And then she would have to send Louis-Marie a thank you and, of course, the "reward." And he would then thank her!

Jamie did in fact have mono. It had been going around his friends. While he spent his days recovering, she watched for the mail every morning.

"Why are you hanging around?" Jamie asked almost rudely. "You're usually out of here at least by noon. You don't have to care for me. I'm not going to die. Not of mono anyway."

"No, it's fine." She may have once admired the legendary Mata Hari but God she hated lying. "You might need something. I have plenty to do anyway. I'm working on a new book. There are so many important scientists I left out of the last one."

Surely it was just adolescence. All those hormones. He had grown much taller in the last months, become extremely good-looking. Like his grandfather, Zack Bowman, he was an excellent athlete. He even had a pretty girlfriend. Katie wondered if they had made love.

CHAPTER 21

BROKEN MORNING

Around two million years ago, Earth entered the Ice Age and thick layers of snow accumulated in the Arctic that compacted into massive sheets of ice. Soon the ice sheets were set into motion under the pressure of their own weight, at which point they became glaciers. Pushing south, the glaciers consumed everything in their path. Boulders, soil, trees—everything but the bedrock was picked up and carried along.
James Kaiser, *Acadia: The Complete Guide*

[I]n the startled space which a youth as lovely as a god has suddenly left forever.
Rainer Maria Rilke, *First Duino Elegy*

An oddity of living with something as terrible as a child's death is that one grasps for the most pathetic things and tries to turn them into consolations. She told herself that he had been with his friends, that he had been having fun diving off that high cliff (over forty feet, someone said), and that the last thing he saw on that Indian summer day was the water in the quarry rising up to meet him, a mirror of autumn trees and blue sky. He must have seen his own reflection rising toward him, he must have dived into his own reflection surrounded by beauty, as though splashing through a picture plane. He couldn't have suffered long (so she told herself), the beer and pot had undoubtedly blunted the blow, the water had stunned him before the rock did, before he drowned.

And thank God it hadn't happened in Maine.

That time of year thou mayst in me behold
When yellow leaves, or none, or few, do hang

Upon those boughs which shake against the cold,
Bare ruined choirs, where late the sweet birds sang.
In me thou see'st the twilight of such day
As sunset fadeth in the west;
Which by and by black night doth take away,
Death's second self, that seals up all in rest.
In me thou see'st the glowing of such fire,
That on the ashes of his youth doth lie,
As the death-bed, whereon it must expire,
Consumed with that which it was nourish'd by.
This thou perceive'st, which makes thy love more strong,
To love that well, which thou must leave ere long.

Her cousin Rex read Shakespeare's 73rd Sonnet at the funeral. Then one of Jamie's friends played "Morning is Broken," Jamie's favorite song, on his guitar. She had surprised herself by insisting that the priest, whom they had only just met, use the old Book of Common Prayer and not the revised one. Jim, holding her hand in the vestry office had agreed this was important. The Book of Common Prayer and the King James Bible. As though only the sixteenth-century words could console them. And in a way the majesty of the old phrases did help.

Would her religious ancestors have understood this horrible event as retribution for her sin?

The house had filled with friends. From all over the college town they came, and after a day or two, from all over the country. Friends, relatives, and cousins—Rex, Martha, and Sebastian. The friends sat, sometimes chatting and laughing quietly, introducing themselves when necessary. They brought casseroles, cookies, cakes, fresh fruit. They made sandwiches.

"You have to eat, Kate, you have to keep your strength up."

Julie and Heather took turns answering the telephone.

The local Episcopal priest who would conduct the service had insisted on praying with her and Nessa. He took them into Nessa's bedroom and made them sit on the bed. He took one of Nessa's hands and told Kate to take the other so the little girl sat between them sniffling. Long streams came out of her nose.

"That stupid priest! I needed a Kleenex and I was trapped. I hate God!" Nessa yelled as soon as he was gone.

Kate took a bottle of bourbon into Jamie's room after supper when all the outsiders had left. She sat on the unmade bed, which still smelled of him. She drank the bourbon and screamed.

"I want my kid! I want my kid back!" she howled over and over, so loud that God should be able to hear her.

Jim knocked on the door.

"Please Katie, we can hear you. For Nessie's sake. Please."

Nancy, who had tactfully taken a room at the local inn during the days leading to the funeral, came and stayed for a while in the guest room. She helped with answering the notes of condolence. She took over many of the household chores, cooking, shopping for food, answering the telephone, deflecting callers' attempts at sympathy, paying the least complicated bills, and bringing the checks to the distracted Kate to sign. She didn't try to talk about what had happened. She had been born too early for the modern addiction to "communication," and she understood that for now words were impotent anyway.

She was wonderful. She was simply "there" and Kate was grateful. But after a week Nancy felt it was time to go, her sad little family had to find its own way.

The sympathy notes kept coming and Kate settled down to answering them. Her favorite was written by an eleven-year-old in a messy attempt at cursive letters: "He was the best Frisbee player I ever knew." Her former art teacher: "There is nothing adequate that one can say," in precise handwriting, India ink on jagged-edged eggshell-colored 100% rag paper. The frilly cards with lilies and religious sentiments from Agnes and other Household people who had worked for her grandmother particularly touched her. Then there was the one from Ian. Even though all he said on the first page of the folded note was "I'm so sorry. I know you gave him a wonderful life," this one she separated from the others and hid.

It wasn't the only thing that Kate hid. Two weeks after Jamie was buried she finally got up the courage to change his bed, to pull off the sheets and pillowcases. She held them to her nose, and yes, they still smelled a little of him. Under his bed she found his diary. She immediately turned to the last page. "My mother is having an affair with some French dude. Dad doesn't know."

For months after Jamie's death Kate moved as though she were catatonic. She felt she was rolling in a glass bubble, afraid it would break and drown her in sorrow. She and Jim and Nessa hardly looked at each other. At first there had been a lot of hugging and she could hear Nessa crying at night. But none of them knew what to say to each other, and each became locked in a private grief. At first Kate continued drinking and Jim began to drink more than he used to.

Then she realized she would become an alcoholic and abruptly stopped. Friends and neighbors tried to say the right things, but they also averted their eyes. Kate understood why no one wanted to come near such a terrible happening. The family felt radioactive.

"You're really good at likenesses," said Jim to her one night out of the blue. They were still wrapped in their separate depressions, they hadn't talked much for months. But still, his face looked different tonight, even worse than usual.

"What do you mean?"

"You know those photos of your coming-out party?"

"You've been looking at my old albums?"

"Particularly one of you dancing with that Canadian guy. You said he was from Montreal. Good-looking guy about your height."

Kate didn't dare answer.

"There are some other photos of him later on. The two of you having a picnic at Vassar. Then some of him playing a guitar, one fooling around with a big dog. Black lab it looks like. He was a big beau of yours if I remember correctly."

"Well, yes, but why are you bringing him up now?"

She shouldn't have asked that. Heart pounding, she waited. She stared at her living room. She noticed the plants she loved, the warbly-glassed windows looking out at the trees, the hundreds of books, the bright colors of the Indian cushions and the contrasting off-white of the slipcovers. She had worked hard to make the pinks, reds, corals, and oranges go together. This inventory she was taking, it was as though her mind was trying to change the subject.

"I was glancing through one of your sketch books I happened to come across. Not meaning to snoop, it's just that I really admire how well you draw."

"Thank you. I don't mind you looking."

He sat down next to her on the sofa. As he did he pulled the small sketchbook out of his back pocket. It was the one she had left in Canada and Louis-Marie had returned. He flipped it open to the last pages. There were two sketches of Ian she'd made that day on the terrace of his house. That they were fine sketches was her first thought, they brought Ian to life in tender lines, they were lovingly drawn. Ian's eyes were looking out of the page at the person who was drawing him. He was smiling.

Kate didn't say anything.

Then Jim flipped back to the front of the book to where there were more sketches, in a more nervous jerky style, of a man sitting on a park bench. There was no mistaking they were of the same person.

"See what I mean? I decided to do a comparison test. And sure enough, they look like the photographs in the album. They're of the same guy, aren't they? The Canadian guy. Only he's older here, you did them recently. In fact the last one is dated this September."

Her mind raced down a list of possible lies. Coincidence. A man on a bus, on a park bench. Same day. Happened to look like Ian. Sketched all those other pages in between all in one day. Yes, it was the old friend. Forgot to tell you I ran into him. Twice.

She couldn't say any of it. She couldn't say anything. She was too exhausted. Her kid was dead. Nothing else mattered. Let Jim go, too. She put her head in her hands. It was an eloquent confession of guilt, the way she sat.

"Good job," he said. "You had me fooled."

Jim moved out the next day. He took a room in the village near the college and she stayed in the house with Nessa.

"Daddy's going to live in town for a while, sweetheart. Just for a while."

Nessa put the knife with the peanut butter on it down on the counter. She poured herself some milk, took the glass and the sandwich to the kitchen table and then sat there without moving. She didn't look at her mother.

"It's been so hard on him. Hard on everybody," began Kate and then she paused. "So it seemed...I mean, he wanted...he wanted some space."

"Space."

"Yes, space. Time to think."

"You guys are getting divorced, right?"

"Oh, no, sweetheart, don't. Not divorce, no, just a little space."

Nessa got up and went to her room. She left the peanut butter and jelly sandwich and the milk on the table. Kate copied out the address and telephone number of the place Jim was renting. She went to Nessa's room and knocked on the closed door.

"Go away," came from the room. Kate pushed the piece of paper under the door and went away.

Grief is creative, almost playful. It hides and then pops out unexpectedly, it changes shapes: a marked-up book, a song, a smelly sneaker, McIntosh apples at the grocery. It continually dons new guises for its attacks. It usurps daily life. It rules.

Kate thought she now understood Halloween better.

She sensed Jim and Nessa were blaming her for everything, maybe even for making Jamie foolhardy.

What had been going on with her and Jamie anyway? Had she been too permissive, had the kids whose company he kept been too fast? Had she guessed they were probably smoking pot, driving too fast, doing other dangerous things and she hadn't tried to stop them? Had she enjoyed Jamie's fool-hardiness? Had she thought of him as a male version of herself? Herself at fifteen? And she remembered the feeling of exhilaration, of daredevil teenage courage.

It was almost comforting to take the blame. She felt herself twelve years old, kneeling in church, praying that Rowdy the Springer spaniel would come and lick her face again.

On she rolled inside her glass bubble, afraid of a wrong move, a twitch, a thought. A thought such as, "How could he not be here, he who was so alive, so noisy, who took up such a big part of the house, of the world, of my life? My son. My son and his sister, the people I love most in the world. How could only one of them still exist?"

And in the swamp that was her mind another thought began to grow, dirtying her grief even further. She had tried to put his diary entry out of her mind but now it grew like some hideous parasite.

"My mother is having an affair with some French dude."

Jamie had known. Jamie had known that his mother had cheated on his father, had driven a wedge between the man and woman who had made him.

The pretty lady with the pink nails she met at the Ritz came back, a clear memory. The lady's hand with the pink nails on her father's forearm. She had been not much older than Jamie then and it had devastated her.

But she had survived and Jamie hadn't. If he had lived she might have made it up to him. She might have shown Jamie, as her parents had shown her, that their marriage could be healed. If it could have been.

Night after night she stayed up reading. She read about geology. The Precambrian period, the Pennsylvanian, the Jurassic. Appalachian. The Taconic orogeny, magma, lithic, tectonic plates. The Bar Harbor Formation. All those layers, all those hundreds and thousands and millions of centuries. Without people. Better without people.

In the Ordovician era the equator went through Montreal.

One night, awake as usual, she found her slippers under the bed and felt her way downstairs to the front hall closet. She didn't like turning lights on. She pulled out the stepladder, ignoring the things that tumbled to the floor of the closet, dragged it to the library and propped it against some shelves. Her hand patted its way across the tops of dusty books until she found where she had hidden Ian's sympathy letter. "Please, anything I can do for you ever, I am here, let me know," he had written in small neat handwriting inside the folded note. She couldn't read it in the moonlight but she had memorized it. He had expected her to hide that note within a note and she had done so. She shuddered, not just from the cold, but from the deceit.

She wanted so much to get in touch with him; she knew how to do it through Louis-Marie. She yearned to be with him in his firelit library again, she ached to be entwined with him. Particularly now that winter had come and the whole world had turned to ice. An *époque glaciare*.

But she did not call or write. She both treasured and hated the fact that she had that option.

She spent Christmas alone. Jim and Nessa went to some friends' house but Kate said she didn't feel like going out, she thought she was "coming down with something." She spent New Year's alone, too.

Nancy, who had been calm and caring from the beginning, said she wished she could come and stay again but Granny

McAllister was sick in Chicago so she needed to go out there to be with her. Granny was over ninety now but her mind was as clear as ever. They had debated whether to tell her about Jamie and had decided they should. If Granny had been devastated she hadn't shown it, but they knew she was hiding a great sadness for her favorite great-grandchild. Now Kate had yet another worry, that Granny's grief may have caused this "turn for the worse."

Nancy called often and Kate found herself putting on a cheerful false voice when she did. At the end of March the call came that Granny had died. The funeral was scheduled for the following weekend.

"Do you want to go?" Kate asked Nessa. "You don't have to, you know. Daddy could come and stay with you while I'm gone."

"I want to go."

Of course she did. Nessa and Jamie and all the great-grandchildren had loved Granny as much as the nine cousins had. How Kate had enjoyed watching her grandmother play with Jamie and Nessa. There it was again: Granny's wiggling middle finger (painted with Windsor nail polish), becoming the neck of a monster made of old fingers. It was crawling toward you, coming to eat you up. And then the poke in the stomach and the child's fit of giggles.

Granny had told the same stories to a new generation, the same stories that she had once told to Katie, Carrie, and their cousins. "And you know what that goat did then?" Of course the children knew what the goat did then, but still they asked, "What? What?" and Granny almost shouted, "That goat ate my brand-new hat!"

And she was the same old lady, now more wrinkled and shrunken, opening her mouth wide in feigned amazement as she listened to a child tell his own story.

Jamie had had long talks with her about crossing the ocean in ships and other curiosities of the old days while Nessa surely remembered her own moments cuddled in the silky lap. Those memories were indelible, they helped to inoculate the children against overwhelming loneliness, helped strengthen them for the calamities that would come.

The forsythia was already in bloom in the McAllister family plot in Graceland, the old cemetery that houses the eternities of Chicago's rich and/or famous.

The family circled the rectangular hole into which Granny McAllister's coffin would be lowered. The relatives were almost all there: Nancy, Aunt Pru, Uncle Oliver, Uncle Peter and his new wife, the nine cousins and most of their spouses, including Carrie and her rich husband, and all the cousins' children. The sensation of there being two people missing was almost a visceral one for Kate, like the irritation one feels when people are lining up for a group portrait and one or two people haven't shown up yet. Of course Jim wouldn't be there, but Jamie, not having Jamie there felt like a cosmic amputation. Nessa was now the oldest of the great grandchildren. Ancient Agnes was there, bent over in her long black coat, her wound-around braid of hair snow white. Elmo, the Chicago chauffeur, and Regina, the cook who used too much garlic, stood off to one side. The family knew Agnes would want to be there and they didn't want to hurt the feelings of the others. Everyone held white roses and Aunt Pru was given credit for the glorious weather. And though there were many who hugged Kate warmly, no one said anything about her troubles.

Someone had made copies of the first stanza of the nautical Hymn #608 from the Episcopal Hymnal and passed them around. It was everyone's favorite hymn, with the possible exception of Granny; family myth had it that as a young woman she had been hit in the head by a jibing boom.

Much as I love the whole song, thought Jim, as he crossed over unnoticed from the drive and stood outside the circle, I hope they only do the first stanza. The McAllister voices rose in the spring air, some squeaky and tremulous, the children's soft but determined, at least two of the older voices strong and competitive. He recognized Martha's and Sebastian's but not Katie's.

"Eternal Father, strong to save, whose arm hath bound the restless wave, who bidd'st the mighty ocean deep...."

"Its own appointed limits keep," thought Kate, and she thought of the beach at Burnmouth.

"Ashes to ashes, dust unto dust," the Presbyterian minister intoned, as the April breeze ruffled what was left of his hair.

Kate felt an arm around her shoulders. Probably her cousin Rex. She turned to smile up at him and saw it was Jim. She reached up to take his hand and then for the first time in weeks she began to cry.

CHAPTER 22

NEW WORLDS AND OLD

In the end, those who were carried off early no longer need us:
They are weaned from the earth's sorrows and joys,
As gently as children outgrow the soft breast or their mothers.
Rainer Maria Rilke, *First Duino Elegy*

"The world's creation did not take place at the beginning of time,
it takes place every day."
Marcel Proust, *In Search of Lost Time: The Fugitive*

Somehow, they put it back together. They did it for Nessa; now that she was an only child, she needed them more than ever. At least that was what they told themselves, easing into it.

They lived with a huge hole in their lives after Jamie died, a huge hole in their family. They didn't discuss it much, and for Kate it felt like a door that wouldn't open. A door she didn't dare open. Hers would have been a perfectly good life had she never known, had she never owned, that wonderful person, her son. She would never have known what she missed, never have known the ebullient, exciting, noisy, always-up-to-something teenager, forever almost sixteen. "He's a real boy, Mrs. Morse," neighbors had said.

The holidays were hard. As a little kid he had loved her Thanksgiving turkey. One year pounding on its tray he had made his high chair jump yelling, "More chicken! More chicken!" Now he was the one who wasn't there in the family group photograph taken at the end of every summer, or on Christmas morning amidst the gift-wrapping litter, the crumpled paper and ribbons on the living room floor.

She found some watercolors of seascapes he had painted that she had never seen before. They were really quite excellent. The sailboats were at angles, there were islands in the background, or perhaps the islands were clouds, turbulent clouds over a rough sea. She had them framed and hung them in the living room.

She gave a thousand dollars to the town library to buy books about the sea. They bought *Captains Courageous* and some how-to-sail books for kids. Get *Moby Dick* and *Lord Jim*, she wanted to tell them. And *Youth*— they must have *Youth*. But she decided to leave them alone to do with the money what they wanted.

For years she dreamed about Jamie. He would be there, exactly himself again, smiling and funny. Sometimes he would be sitting at the kitchen table, sometimes somewhere else. She would apologize, promise to be a better mother. "We'll have fun again. I promise." Once she asked him where he'd been all these years. "Florida" he answered.

She tried to think of him as little as possible.

One night Nessa was upstairs doing her homework and Kate and Jim lingered over their wine at the kitchen table. It was the kind of table that city people loved, a heavy oak country table, scarred and tough. Kate kept flowers in a heavy earthenware jug on it always, and now they were lilacs. Lilacs with their evocative aroma, better than Proust's madeleine.

"I knew about him all along," said Jim. "Well, I didn't know you'd spent time recently," he took a gulp of wine, "but I knew about him years ago. I knew what he did to you."

"What do you mean, what he did to me?"

"Swept you off your feet. Changed your life. Made it impossible for any of the rest of us to ever measure up."

"Oh, Jim."

"Made you quit going to the deb parties. Drove your father nuts."

"How did you know all that?"

"People talked. You were famous in those days, you know. All the boys had crushes on you. Wanted to dance with you, take you out. Then all of a sudden you were out of bounds. You changed. People said someone had broken your heart, some Canadian Jew whose grandfathers were multimillionaires."

"You've never told me any of this."

"Well, I didn't exactly want to remember it. I'd hoped you'd forgotten him."

She didn't say anything. She was tired of lying.

After a while she got up and stood behind him. She bent down and nuzzled her face in the side of his beard. It was as though she wasn't ready to meet him head-on. He reached up a big freckled hand and played with her hair.

"Give me a hug," he said.

"I love you," she sniffled. And he pulled her into his lap.

Out of what was left Kate slowly constructed a new world.

Nancy's voice was clear and steady on the telephone. Nancy, the woman who could navigate by the stars.

"I don't know how to tell you this, precious," Nancy began, and Kate, far away in New Hampshire, shuddered. Kate felt she now lived in a fragile world, a world built on volcanic fault lines, and she didn't think she could stand yet another disaster. She held her breath and waited.

"Burnmouth has been sold," said her mother.

She explained that Uncles Peter and Oliver had taken the decision upon themselves; Nancy and Pru hadn't been consulted because this was the province of men.

"Forty thousand," said Nancy. "They sold it to pay the taxes."

"No," said Kate, in almost a whisper. "No!"

"That new motel across Eden Street bought it so they can have a view of the bay."

"A view of the bay? How can they see the bay from across Eden Street?" Kate remembered the horrible irony of the motel being built where her tree-stump castle had been.

"Apparently they plan to cut down the trees in between," said Nancy, and her voice trembled ever so slightly.

Her woods, her childhood woods. Kate didn't say anything. Nancy went on.

"I know. I'm furious. I did what I could. I called Granny's great friend Winifred White, I had some vague idea, not a very well thought-out one I'll admit, but I called Mrs. White thinking she might lend us some money until we could come up with a better solution. Maybe have a charitable institution take it over, or even a nursing home."

"Yes, what did she say?"

"Bless her heart, the old dear said she would buy it herself immediately for a hundred thousand dollars cash."

"But that's wonderful!"

"It was too late," said Nancy. "The papers had been signed. Nobody would budge."

They both paused.

"Perhaps it's just as well," said her mother. "Who of us could have kept up such a big house in this day and age? Think of all the people Granny had working for her."

"The Household," said Katie. "I know. But still...."

The next summer Kate visited Burnmouth. It was July 1977, and she decided to go there on the thirtieth, knowing there would be a blue moon that night. It was her silly tribute to superstition; blue moons had usually been lucky for her. Or maybe not. Anyway, she didn't have to tell anyone that she nursed these vestiges of childhood.

There was a chain across the driveway so she had to get out of her car to remove it. Weeds poked up through the gravel. The grass in the circle was becoming a meadow, and some of the shutters on the house were askew. Indoors, the house, naked without its family and furniture, was hot and dusty. The smell was almost familiar but not quite, there was still perhaps a touch of wood smoke.

She went immediately to the telephone closet. Of course the coats and umbrellas were gone, and the phone too, but on the wall were the growth statistics from three generations of McAllister cousins.

She took a deep breath and resolved that she would be strong. It was all here, in this hot tomblike space, all the evidence of an earlier civilization. Here were the hooks where the jacket Carrie wore in pretend weddings had hung, as well as the odd smelling sou'wester gear that almost kept them dry sailing on windy days. Here was the hole where the telephone had hung, the telephone on which she'd invited Ian to the party. Now useless wires covered with brown fur dangled from a hole in the plaster. She saved for last her scrutiny of the smudged markings where the children (and dogs) had tried to hold still while grown-up hands steadied books on their heads and recorded their heights. She picked out Jamie's height when he was twelve, almost exactly level with Katie's when she was twelve. Apparently she had stopped growing after that but he had grown for almost four more years. He must have been at least five ten or eleven when he died.

But she had begun to shake and her eyes to burn. She knew she couldn't stay any longer. Nor did she want to see any more of the house. As she left she averted her eyes from the French doors that led to the veranda and its glowing view of the lawn, the beach, and the bay.

Afterward she visited the house only in her dreams. Many, many dreams that went on for years.

Not long after that Kate learned that the new motel had boarded chambermaids and waitresses in Granny's house until the town cited it as a fire hazard. Then, so the tourists could get an ocean view for their one or two nights, the owners tore down the house, bulldozed the woods and gardens; chopped down the cedar hedge and the huge oak tree where the children's swing had swung. The only parts the motel owners couldn't obliterate were the rocks and the children's Pretend Town. Only time could do that.

Farther up the beach the ferry to Nova Scotia was doing a brisk business.

Like everyone over the age of fifteen, Kate's life had been moving faster and faster. Now in middle age, it tumbled along at a rapid clip and, of course, soon it would go even faster.

Nessa finished her childhood as an only child. It was hard on her because she had worshipped her brother, but she got through it and married, and had children of her own. Soon Kate was happy sitting on the floor with her three grandchildren, using blunt scissors to cut red, yellow, blue, green, and orange paper into circles, trapezoids, spirals, squiggles, and confetti. To Eleanor, her only granddaughter, she promised Granny's diamond bracelet when Eleanor married or when Kate died, whichever came first.

Eventually Jim and Kate were glad they had managed to stay married and they settled into a kind of comforting domesticity. All the gentle homespun chores wrapped Kate in a lumpy blanket of happiness; she saved chicken bones for soup, garbage for compost, old bed sheets for rags. She made stews and froze them, she actually cleaned the refrigerator shelves. She nursed her plants through the winters and Jim helped her carry them outside in the spring. She read a great deal, less science now, more novels.

She continued to paint, and in the back of her mind were hopes of making another children's science book someday. She produced landscapes and still-lives, and when her grandchildren visited they painted with her.

Lingering over their bottle of wine every night after dinner, she and Jim talked as they had when they were young, about books, politics, ecology, and now, memories. Jim talked the most; he no longer had students to listen to him and teaching had been his life. Now he puttered around the house, joined committees, complained more than he used to.

Kate never went to Quebec again. She wrote Ian a polite

little letter, a sort of thank-you note almost, and he answered her with a concise, "I understand."

Jim died of a stroke the morning after the party they gave to celebrate their fortieth anniversary.

Kate knew he had still been inching his way through Finnegan's Wake, and when she came back from the cemetery she noticed it on the night stand open to page 292. Sitting down on the bed that still held his odor she read, "Plutonic lovliaks twinnt Platonic yearlings—you must, how, in undivided reawlity draw the line somewhawre." She sat there for a long time, her eye following without comprehending the strange words, ignoring the people downstairs who had come home with her so she wouldn't be alone.

At first Jim's death had seemed an extension of his life. So many friends and family comforting her, and the planning of the memorial (people reading Joyce and Conrad) had distracted her; the hundreds of tributes from students and others had made her proud.

But Kate's grief was immense, different from that for Jamie, but just as devastating. It was grief dressed in yet another costume and as the days crawled on it got worse. She knew that, unlike the horrible expression, "Death is a part of life," death was the sharp clanging shut of a steel door, like the door to a freight elevator, and not only was there was no reopening it, there was an abyss on the other side.

Kate's mind felt mired in a mud hole, above which superficial thoughts became like feathers in a breeze. She lost things, forgot things, repeated things. She got sick. As though she needed to be reminded that she would die too, her body kept calling for attention with aches and itches and coughs, sleeplessness and restlessness. And exhaustion. Alone in the empty house, she felt she could hardly push the boulder of the day along; at night she couldn't face the dark, couldn't face the bed.

And embedded in the days and nights were all the regrets, large and small. Now that Jim was gone the regrets tumbled out all over the place like poisoned candy from a monster piñata.

Of course she regretted the petty marital squabbles, but even more Kate regretted her gradual drawing away from sex with Jim. Nightly back rubs became their closest physical intimacy, yet her fingers had been reluctant to touch his moist skin; she'd insisted on feeling his flesh through fabric.

The largest regret, of course, was her affair with Ian. How could she have hurt Jim so? Wonderful Jim who had loved her so much, and had been so good to her; her thanks had been to hurt him. How must he have felt when he learned she'd run off right from under his nose?

Yet all the time she'd felt with Jim a layer of contentment that was now gone: a thin but buoyant and warm layer of marital happiness. Her world, her whole existence had floated on that layer of happiness.

And there was more. There was Jamie. The question would always be there, like an inoperable tumor or a bullet near the spine: had her son's knowing of her adultery disturbed his equilibrium? Was she to some extent responsible for what had happened to him?

After Granny died Nancy had moved to a leafy suburb outside of Chicago and now she invited Kate to visit her. A little money from the old days had dribbled down through the correct lineup of family deaths, and Kate was happy that her mother had found a certain amount of luxury again. Nancy's charming old coach house was close to the homes of some of her old bridesmaids and with these friends she played bridge on Tuesday and Thursday afternoons, and went into town to the symphony on Fridays.

For ten days Nancy and Kate chatted and shopped. They ate lunches at Nancy's lovely club in a sunny room with huge languid flowers painted on the walls. Nancy and Kate peeked in to see the oval ballroom, its skinny black and gold pillars entwined with roses for an evening party. Nancy poked Kate's arm and said, "This is where you would have gone to all those coming out parties!" and they both laughed.

Kate was impressed by how her mother and her friends lived. They reminded her that she had always had what people called "role models," and she tried to draw sustenance from the vibrancy of these old ladies.

They didn't seem to complain much or discuss their ailments; apparently they considered the unpleasantries of life not suitable for conversation. They obviously continued to care how they looked and how the little worlds they lived in looked. They went to the hairdresser once a week and had their nails done and when it became absolutely necessary they resorted to wigs. They forfeited bits of their noses to the surgeon's scalpel and wore Band-Aids to cocktail parties where they asked for vodka instead of gin because they heard it was better for you. You could tell they tried to avoid dowager humps though it was difficult for some, leaning over aluminum walkers. Some of them tried assisted living facilities, though more than one couldn't stand the décor, the food, or the boredom and moved back into smaller apartments. When their chauffeurs were gone, or they couldn't pass the driving test, they learned public transportation. They didn't resign from their clubs and they played bridge for as long as their short-term memories allowed. They may not have had careers, thought Kate, who had once wanted a career so badly, but they did have a kind of work and they did it well, and with dignity.

Kate felt as well a new kinship with the ghosts of her grandmother, Mrs. Andover White, and Margaret Louise van Linden. Members of Granny's Household should be role models too: Agnes and Hermione and many others over the years. Where was Agnes now, she wondered. Perhaps she had gone back to Ireland, perhaps she lived alone in some quiet boarding house. Perhaps she was dead. Kate wished she had been kinder to the old lady, had kept up. Kate's family owed her so much.

And of course, there was Nancy.

She wondered what Nancy must have felt when Zack had died. She, Kate, had gone back to her nice husband, children, and house in New Hampshire (and of course to her secret love affair), and Nancy had gone back to an empty apartment and the task of cleaning up Zack's mess. What had Nancy thought about going through those stacks of photos of expensive horses and pretty women? What had she thought about her own marriage, so flawed and yet so important to her?

Kate had never asked.

And then a few months later Kate had to make another trip to Chicago.

The suburban hospital had flowered wallpaper in all the rooms. The colors were summer-bedroom colors, and the paraphernalia necessary to sickness was disguised or downplayed as much as possible. Through the organdy-curtained windows Kate could see green leaves dancing cheerily in the sunlight.

Nancy's head, her face swollen from steroids, lay round and wrinkleless on the white pillow. She looked as she had in pictures taken on a French beach some eighty years earlier. She reached out a thin arm to Kate.

"Terrific!" she said in a croaking voice, and Kate knew that Nancy was telling her how happy she was that Kate had come.

They had a few silent days together before Nancy went into a coma. She didn't die right away, just seemed to sleep.

As Kate watched her mother breathe she remembered how as children she and Carrie needed to be "tucked in" every night. "Good night, ladies, good night ladies, good night LADIES, I'm going to eat you up!" At the end of the song Nancy would bury her face against their small squirming, giggling, blanket-cocooned bodies.

Now in the pretty hospital Kate listened for the footsteps of the nurses. When she was sure they were out of earshot, very softly she tried to sing to Nancy the songs that Nancy had sung to her. Kate's favorite was "Lili Marlene," and she suspected it was Nancy's favorite too. She wondered if her mother had ever sung it to her father. She wondered if Zack had ever noticed how loving and charming Nancy could be. She wondered if, when Nancy McAllister was young and beautiful, he had desired her for herself, or if she had always been a transparent phantom and his real love had been Burnmouth. Burnmouth and all it represented.

CHAPTER 23

THE SMELL OF PINE AND THE SEA

[Our] faces marked by toil, by deceptions, by success, by love; our weary eyes looking still, looking always looking anxiously for something out of life, that while it is expected is already gone— has passed unseen, in a sigh, in a flash—together with the youth, with the strength, with the romance of illusions.
Joseph Conrad, *Youth*

For decades the McAllisters had gathered in Chicago the first Thursday of every April for their "family meeting," their meeting to discuss their real estate holdings in Chicago and elsewhere. Cousins and their spouses arrived from England, Ireland, France, and Italy. Often Kate, with or without Jim, had gone too. The summer cousins—some combination of Rex, Martha, Petey, Fred, Mary, Sarah, and Sebastian—were usually there. Carrie sometimes came. It was the only time that Kate could see her far-flung relatives and she always loved the crazy coziness of it.

In spite of Aunt Pru's efforts the weather was almost always dreadful; the English cousins almost always got mugged or put in fear of its happening. How wonderfully exotic these English cousins were with their strange haircuts, their bad teeth, their tweedy clothes, and their mumbly voices! Most exotic of all was elegant old Cousin Darlington in his striped trousers, an almost horizontal watch chain looped across his waistcoat. He and Zack had once taken her out into the corridor and tried to teach her how to walk when she was a teenager ("toe out, toe out!"). His beautiful, very rouged, much younger wife, an opera singer from New Zealand, boasted a long shelf of marcelled blonde hair that fascinated them all. For a time there had been Grandpa in his wheelchair, and his tiny old sisters. They included dotty Aunt Priscilla, who collected antique clothes, such as infanta christening dresses she found in the Pyrenees, and Aunt Mabel, whose posture reminded one of a clipper ship under sail. Very rich cousins from New York came, and medium-rich ones from Philadelphia.

Around a long table they sat, each confronted by a collection of mimeographed pieces of paper. In spite of their different outfits and hairdos, one could see that most of them had the same "ski-jump" noses, square chins, and long fingers. The women knitted or worked their needlepoint, and the younger cousins giggled and whispered. On the handouts with their lists of numbers Kate sketched cartoon portraits as discreetly as she could and passed notes to Rex. As the years went on and Kate's cousins matured, Martha, the most conscientious, became their leader, and after her own work as a lawyer in Washington grew too voluminous, Sebastian took over.

A day of listening to managers' reports, lawyers' warnings, and trustees' harangues was always mercifully interrupted at midpoint by a cart jiggling with ice bucket and bottles of gin, vodka, and Bloody Mary mix being wheeled in. Carefully labeled sandwiches and soft drinks followed. After lunch, empty chairs were pushed out of the way as some of the women decided shopping gave deeper meaning to their lives than real estate. An occasional snore was heard. Toward 5:30 people looked at their wristwatches and realized they had less than an hour to put their feet up, change, and find a cab during rush hour to take them to the Racquet Club or the Casino or some other elegant club. Certainly what had sustained many throughout the long day was looking forward to a delicious dinner, champagne, and wittily naughty toasts made by those who were famous for making them. (Darlington, of course, and Zack in the old days, and later Rex and Sebastian.) They also looked forward to the much-repeated family stories and the moment when the New York cousins would stand up and sing Cole Porter and Noel Coward songs like "Miss Otis Regrets" and "Don't Put Your Daughter on the

Stage, Mrs. Worthington." Everyone loved and was amazed by this annual performance; how did they remember all those words for all those years!

But those days were gone now. Whether it was family members squabbling, or just economics stumbling into new configurations, eventually there were no more April meetings. And as the relatives had scattered across the map the way American families do, there was no magnetic Burnmouth to draw Granny's progeny together in the summers. The youngest McAllisters hardly knew one another. Nessa's children and the others of their generation lived in different cities; Christmas cards were as close as anyone got to "staying in touch."

All Kate's cousins were old now, and her only sibling had died. Carrie had had breast cancer for years. It had once been thought taken care of, but two years ago it had come back and, in spite of all the horrible medical things they do to people, she had died, her lovely hair gone for no good reason. And Sebastian had ALS; each time Kate visited, his muscles seemed to have melted further, and his words had sunk further into verbal sludge. But he remained cheerful, grateful for what he had left, and he never stopped joking.

Perhaps because of often laughing over the phone with wonderfully silly and irreverent Sebastian, Kate finally felt she must not give in to endless sadness. Ever the instigator, she decided there should be a McAllister family reunion. It would include the new children and grandchildren and it should be in Chicago. Chicago had been Granny and Grandpa's city, the McAllister city where square-bearded ancestors had once made a fortune—a fortune long gone. Besides, that was where Sebastian and his wife, Sue, lived.

Kate wrote to her cousins. "Come to Chicago so we can all meet again and remember Burnmouth. And do you have any pictures we can use for decorations, or stories we can tell?"

Acceptances arrived from Washington, Boston, New York, Pennsylvania, New Hampshire, and Indiana. Copies of old photographs came, too. There were pictures from even before the cousins were born: beautiful young Granny with her heavy-lidded eyes, tiny Nancys, Prus, and Peters in their starched summer clothes and little white shoes, the goat cart with the hat-eating goat, fluffy dogs, babies (who could that one be?) held by bigger children. There was adolescent Katie, out of scale to the others, trying to pull the hem of her dress over her knees. The Pretend Town of the beach could be seen in many of the backgrounds. Kate made place cards and posters out of the pictures. She collected reminiscences and produced an illustrated booklet.

In Chicago Kate and Sue arranged a dinner at Uncle Peter's old club. It wasn't one of the fancy clubs that Granny and Grandpa had belonged to, of which Grandpa had been a founding member, where they had gone after the old meetings. This was a club once-famous architects and businessmen had frequented, but now its leather furniture had become threadbare and shabby.

At dinner Kate told the others how, years before, she had gone to see Burnmouth after it was sold but still standing, and how sad it had made her to see what had happened to it.

"For a while the motel people had their maids and waitresses sleep there. They used it as a dormitory."

"Imagine, Granny's house as a dormitory!"

Several people reacted in horror.

"It was always a disgrace," said Martha, preferring a tangential outrage. "Imagine Granny's poor servants sleeping up on the third floor where it was so hot and airless."

"Perhaps they put beds in the dining room under the chandelier!"

Some people tittered.

"No, I mean in our day!" persisted Martha. "When we were living there, Granny's maids, they all slept up there under the eaves! It was a fire trap, it was disgraceful."

"Hardly any windows," said Rex.

Several of the cousins had been there recently, long after Kate's visit.

"There's an elegant sort of hotel been built since," said Sarah. "Bob and I had dinner there last summer."

"Could you recognize the view?" asked Kate.

"Yes, actually I could. From what used to be the dining room. I could see the beach and I think I recognized a birch tree. There was a piano player and it was really quite a nice evening."

"I don't think I could ever go there again," said Kate. "It would kill me."

"All right," announced Martha, taking charge of the situation, as she often did. "Let's have some reminiscences. Mary!" She pointed to Mary, thus interrupting her whispering to Petey. "You haven't said much this evening."

Mary took her time.

"When Granny used to smoke," she said slowly, "I was transfixed by how long the ash could grow without dropping."

"Exactly," exclaimed her sister Sarah. "That's perhaps my strongest image of Granny."

"And remember what's-her-name, the maid with the braid on her head—"

"Agnes!" several shouted out.

"How strict she was," said Fred. "She terrified me."

They laughed at the idea of enormous middle-aged Fred being terrified.

"Remember 'Passengers will please refrain?'"

"And when the pig got loose!"

"How about the time Petey fell in the chowder!"

"To me, Burnmouth will always mean the smell of pine and the sea," said Rex wistfully, quieting them all.

Sebastian had sat grinning through all this and now he managed to raise a shaking finger towards his mouth; Kate, sitting next to him, knew he wanted to tell a story. She clinked her spoon on her champagne glass and Rex, on her other side, clinked his and soon the long table was silenced and everyone turned toward the big man folded into the mechanized chair.

189

"Never...much time with my old man," he began very slowly. "Lived with Mother in Connecticut...saw Dad in summers."

The cousins waited.

"Best time ever had with Dad." Sebastian was smiling a crooked smile and his eyes were twinkling. "Went to a movie together...British commandoes canoeing down a river...blow up a German ship. Dad was a great canoe-er."

"God, yes," interrupted Martha. "Uncle Peter's canoe!! Will you ever forget it?"

The cousins made assenting noises.

"So Dad and I decided...attack the ferry. Ferry to Nova Scotia. It was night...we paddled over, threw firecrackers up. The sailors threw lit cigarettes down at us.... Like tracer bullets in the dark...."

Sebastian stopped, so they assumed he was through. They laughed, clapped, and cheered, of course, but then they were still. No one spoke for a long time. Kate closed her eyes and shut out the festive table with its flowers, candles, silverware, and messy dishes. She stopped seeing the faces, arms, and torsos of her beloved family. Instead she seemed to see the river Thames at dusk in a book she had loved; Marlow was ending his story of the Congo. It was a different story of course, there had been no evil Kurtz, the McAllisters were at worst unwitting colonists. She couldn't help herself, she couldn't ignore it, the foreboding was so strong: it was as though Sebastian was about to lead them all "into the heart of an immense darkness."

CHAPTER 24

GOOGLE EARTH

She had reached old age with all of her nostalgias intact....
She went on living in the static and marginal time of memories.
Gabriel Garcia Marquez, *One Hundred Years of Solitude*

Dear Katie, now that you're almost eighty you can legitimately claim Granny's mantle. Have a great birthday." On the front of the card, from Rex in Indiana, was a drawing of an eighteenth-century duchess.

It made her laugh—and also shudder. Kate felt that, no matter her age, she would never be as old as Granny. She refused to cut her long gray hair or throw away her high heels and even hoped she might date again. Inspecting the photos of recently dead businessmen in the *NY Times* obituaries she laughed at herself for evaluating them. Some in their seventies and eighties didn't look so bad. Maybe there was someone out there, someone like Jim or Ian, someone who would change her life again.

And though she was now chronologically as old Granny, unlike Granny she had no dominion such as Burnmouth over which to reign. It wasn't a regal mantle that she had inherited, but there was, she felt sure, something (besides the diamond bracelet), something else to which she was heir. She wondered what it was.

The familiar beauty of her New Hampshire town was being nibbled away by developers, and the deadly quarry she only sometimes dared drive by was like a sinkhole that might swallow her, too, so she had sold her house and moved to an apartment in Boston.

It was a small apartment, minimalist, spare because she had brought with her only some of her favorite furniture from New Hampshire. There was a guest room big enough for Nessa and Gregg and their children, and a tiny room with a window and north light where she hoped to finally finish her second children's book. An old bedroom table was just big enough to hold a sheet of Arches paper taped down at the sides; she kept her paints and water on what used to be a nightstand.

For a long time the paper remained blank while she researched Louis Agassiz and his studies of glaciers. She wondered if she would dare try to contact Ian when she finished the illustration, she wondered if he would remember having suggested the *époque glaciare* that night in New York. This book, supposedly a sequel to the first, seemed to be taking forever. Jim's death had slowed her down, it was as though he had taken a part of her with him.

Easily distracted, she would glance out over the parking lot to the rain-spattered Charles River and think of Aunt Pru. Would Pru have taken credit for the erratic new climate? Crazy Aunt Pru, who let the children believe she controlled the weather. The weather, thought Kate, that great metaphor inside of which we all live.

She looked forward to the evenings when dark blotted out the river and lights in the surrounding buildings came on. She had ordered a case of Moët et Chandon Champagne the first day and she drank a third of a bottle each night. A month later she ordered another case.

After supper, surrounded by unpacked boxes and plants still without saucers, she read for hours beside her glass of champagne the diamond bracelet on her wrist.

Luckily she still had the bracelet. Years before, tipsy after a party, she had tied it to a helium balloon and dangled it from her little finger against the night sky. Only one of the many stupid things she had done in her life, but still, she always smiled when she remembered.

Occasionally the radio played music that brought her to her feet. Once an Oldies station played "Blue Moon," and she twirled around the apartment, bumping into tables and chairs, counters and appliances. She treasured these bits of happiness, encouraged by champagne and nostalgia.

It was hard being old, however, and Kate fumed against the new world, particularly the digital world that had replaced her own. She thought the digital world boring and unromantic. She imagined algorithms crawling like giant spiders; someday they would devour every human endeavor and nothing natural would remain. Passivity would atrophy people, turning them into mindless creatures for whom everything was done, who could do nothing on their own even if they wanted to. Worst of all, "hooking up" had replaced making love.

Kate, all alone now, was able to ignore a large part of this beeping, distracting, interrupting new world; she could avoid its semi-comatose people with heads bent over tiny, lighted rectangles. She made no effort to embrace the new toys, no effort to "keep up" or "fit in."

But she did look up things on Google now and then, and that was how she learned that Ian had died.

The man she had loved since she was on the edge of adult life, the man for whom she had hurt her husband, for whom she had perhaps hurt her son even more; he was gone. Now in her banishment, exiled from even her faintest hopes, she would remove herself from the yearnings of people for each other, their passions, needs, sorrows, and happiness; all of that would exist only in books.

Wrapping herself in a cloak of words, Kate read. Sometimes she perused a nineteenth-century English novel she should have read years before, sometimes she wandered listlessly through a contemporary short story or memoir. Sometimes she read histories of science and marveled at the men (seldom women) who had attempted to figure out the universe. Sometimes she indulged in fashion magazines, or the pornography of medical journalism. Often she explored the byways of the Norton Anthology, happy to rediscover forgotten phrases

("Stumbling on melons, as I pass, ensnared with flowers, I fall on grass"). In and out of thickets of paragraphs she made her way, her companions all those writers and poets who had cared so about life and death and love and now were dead and gone. She reread Jim's essays, his volume on Conrad.

Often she would put her book down and just think her own thoughts. She had never done so much thinking in her life; it was as though, now that she was old, she was trying to construct an accurate picture of the world, and to fit her oddly shaped life into an immense jigsaw puzzle.

She even dared to let thoughts of Jamie back into her life. Thoughts, memories and questions. What sort of man would he have become? Would he have married, given her grandchildren? Helped her move into the new apartment? Carried the bigger boxes, help her set up the computer?

When spring came again Kate began to feel less sad. Whiffs of memories floated up unbidden; a smell, a taste, an aura of a place charmed her.

Then memories of Burnmouth crystallized, memories of those summers that were her legacy. Those summers had gone on so long, half her life it seemed; their details so real, so vivid, she saw them as through calm, clean, sunlit water.

Sometimes, when she closed her eyes, she thought she heard a familiar sound, that sort of swishing sound that had puzzled and enchanted Katie when she was a child. It was slightly rhythmic, almost like breathing. Possibly it was the wavelets inhaling and exhaling upon the pebble beach, perhaps the wind dancing in the leaves, or maybe a car taking the curves as it crunched down the gravel driveway.

Letting her body go limp as though on warm rocks, finally there were no sharp edges, only the sun, the breeze, the ocean, and the seagulls crying. She had been happy, now she was happy again, and she hadn't a doubt in the world that the rocks underneath her would stay just as they were forever.

ACKNOWEDGEMENTS

I would like to thank my editor Carolyn Currie, who worked tirelessly on all aspects of the manuscript for several years. No matter what else was happening in her busy life, she found time for my endless questions and problems. I'm grateful to many others who gave valuable advice and encouragement or helped in other ways: Barbara Bogosian, David Burnham, Shoshannah Cohen, Bonnie Gibbons, Jock Heron, Keith Lorenz, Joanne Omang, Sandy Righter, Alane Rollings, and Bill Schmidt.

I also want to thank the wonderful Maine Authors Publishers who patiently made this book possible.

If Ted Cohen were here I would thank him for his astute comments and most of all, for his belief in me.

Because my novel is full of quotations from works I've loved, I also have many to thank for permissions to borrow from published works.

First of all I'd like to thank Michael Chabon, and James Kaiser who kindly let me use excerpts from their works. I'm grateful to Daniel Post Senning for helping me with quotations from the 1922 edition of Emily Post's Etiquette. Many publishers gave permissions to use excerpts from works to which they control the rights. They are as follows:

Excerpt from LETTERS TO A YOUNG POET by Rainer Maria Rilke, translated by M. D. Herter Norton. Copyright ©1934, 1954 by W.W. Norton & Company, Inc. renewed ©1962, 1982 by M.D. Herter Norton. Used by permission of W.W. Norton & Company, Inc.

Excerpt from "Cut Grass" from THE COMPLETE POEMS OF PHILIP LARKIN by Philip Larkin, edited by Archie Burnett Copyright © 2012 by The Estate of Philip Larkin. Reprinted by permission of Farrar, Straus and Giroux.